What The Butler Saw

Catherine Harman

ISBN: 978-1-326-53203-1

PublishNation
www.publishnation.co.uk

Chapter One

The alarm went off. Sara groaned; she really didn't like Mondays and she certainly didn't like term time Mondays. They heralded the onset of a quintet of lonely nights without Hugo that spread out before her like a lonely, hollow void with only a fading memory of the beautifully romantic weekend they had just shared. This weekend had been particularly lovely as they had been planning the pre Christmas party that Hugo threw annually. Even lovelier, they had been shopping for a new dress for her to wear to it!

Catapulting herself back into her studies and university life after living it up in London was always both a disappointment and a culture shock. She thought back to a time when it hadn't been like this; she had been excited, enthused, passionate even, about her chemistry degree. She smiled as she remembered being enthralled and fascinated by the composition of matter, inducing chemical reactions and witnessing the interactions between atoms. That keenness and rapture had lasted nearly a whole academic year and since then she had sulkily endured, rather than enjoyed, her continuing education. She would actually have seriously considered leaving University despite her reluctance to accept personal failure had she been brave enough to tell her parents; but she wasn't. She just couldn't do it to them after all they'd done for her and knowing how proud they were. It would be bad enough for them that she probably wouldn't use her degree once she had escaped the uni's clutches but at least she would have it and, more importantly, her parents would know she had it.

So she doggedly continued pretty much counting the days down. She was extremely fortunate that, as her only real interest was Hugo now, whilst she was no longer thrilled by matter and energy, she was innately and extraordinarily skilled in the subject. Now in her final year, it would soon be over and if things panned out the way she hoped for and expected, she would shortly be kept in the manner to which she would like to become accustomed. She could hardly wait to move to Redcliffe Square in South Kensington with its elegant wrought iron railinged green and graceful town houses and into Hugo's beautiful big home where she had been spending more and more weekends over the last few months. She touched the snooze on her iPhone for a second...and third time, snuggled deeper and deeper into the cosy cocoon of her duvet and imagined life as Mrs Bradley-Smethurst.

She had met her handsome beau in the little Costa in Cabot Circus. It had been a Saturday in late spring and she could remember the excitement she'd felt as she'd embarked on her shopping expedition to Bristol. She had had £65 in her purse which, in those days, had been a fortune to her so she'd taken herself off and caught the train to Broadmead. Cabot Circus had only been a short walk from the station and she'd been able to browse all the shops along the way. Once at the lovely modern mall, she'd gone into every single one of the shops on two thirds of the lower tier like the preverbal child in a sweet shop before feeling in need of a sit down and a cup of tea; she had chosen the Costa. Hugo had already been in there eating a chocolate muffin and drinking from a giant mug of coffee. Just like in the movies, their eyes had met and it had been like the whole world had stopped. She didn't think she'd ever seen anyone so gorgeous. He'd been with two friends and they were surrounded by lots of bags of stuff they'd all purchased, mainly, it had looked, from sports shops.

He had evidently felt the same as she because he hadn't taken his eyes off her, though she had, of course, played it as coolly as possible. When his friends had stood up to leave, he'd nervously scribbled something on his paper napkin and gently pushed it into her hand as they'd all walked past her table and away into the outside world. Her eyes had followed his tall, athletic body until he had been out of sight and then she'd timidly read the note. It had said exactly what she'd been hoping, but had barely dared to dream of. There had been simply a mobile number and a scribbled 'PLEASE call me, Hugo x'. Her heart had skipped a beat..or three. Hugo had admitted the following week when he'd come to Exeter to see her that he'd

2

never, ever done anything as forward before but had been so overwhelmed by her beauty that he had been able to force himself to overcome his lack of confidence where the fairer and infinitely more complicated sex were involved and make that unprecedented step.

Shit! How was it that time already? She had a lecture at 10am and was going to be late. Again. She leapt out of bed, stubbing her toe in the process and, swearing again, threw herself into the shower. There wasn't time for hair washing and she was pulling on skinny jeans and sweater over her petite body just ten minutes later. A quick glance in the mirror indicated the necessity of scraping her blonde hair into a bobble and she was good to go.

. . . .

It was time for Hugo's second drink of the day. At eight o'clock every Monday to Friday morning he had a strong, milky coffee made with the Gaggia espresso machine in a brown earthenware mug. For the past eight months it had had to be decaffeinated due to his doctor's orders following the worrying heart palpitations he had been experiencing.

At ten o'clock he had an Earl Grey in the blue Wedgewood. Rupert, who had implemented this routine, enjoyed looking after the Master. He was aware, of course, that Hugo didn't like being addressed as such but it pleasantly amused Rupert and somehow made him feel more important. He felt it was seemly and correct as in his mind he saw himself as a 'man servant' or 'butler' circa 1920. To avoid the Master's wrath, this preferred title was usually reserved only for his own musings. Rupert enjoyed his job, it suited him very well. He had originally been employed officially when both he and Hugo had graduated from Bristol University. His responsibility at that time had been to complete any necessary computer and paperwork associated with the Master's business but over the years in this employment, his role had grown into the function of full Personal Assistant.

. . . .

Hugo was enjoying his tea. He sighed contentedly; what a truly lucky man he was. Not only did he have the most beautiful, intelligent and adorable girlfriend in the world and indeed the best life generally but he also had a PA who made the best ever cup of tea! It never tasted quite the same when he made it for himself. Continuing on with his reflections on the theme of his good fortune, he looked around his lovely room, thought of all the splendid things in his very pleasant life and sighed happily again.

Very slightly taller than his tea maker, more muscular and with a somewhat unruly mop of strawberry blond hair, permanently ruddy cheeks and an affable smile never far from his lips, Hugo was considered by most to be a very handsome man. His comfortable and gentle demeanour endeared people to him; they trusted and liked him. And with good reason as he was an honest, sincere and considerate man. If he had a fault at all; it was that he could sometimes be too easy going, too trusting and too naive leaving him in a position in which he could be taken advantage of. Fortunately the people with whom he came into contact were nice too so occurrences of that nature seldom took place enabling him to pass through life with ease and comfort. The silver spoon with which he had been born had no doubt helped but his parents had brought him up not only to count his blessings but to also ignore setbacks. This positive and grateful approach certainly seemed to be working for him.

. . . .

Rupert had not enjoyed the weekend. He had not enjoyed a single weekend since the Sara creature had come onto the scene and monopolised them. During the week he felt useful, needed even and because of that, relatively fulfilled but on Saturdays and Sundays he felt cut adrift, without purpose and lost.

He had filled the lonesome past two days cleaning and organising the kitchen and bathrooms, dodging in and out, as he did so, to avoid feeling that he were in the Master's and *her* way. Even though the

4

two days which most people liked best were not pleasant for him, he was however looking forward to the party weekend in two weeks time. Whist it was completely true that he hated the intrusion, noise and fuss, he did like to coordinate evenings that his master would enjoy and be proud of. Hugo was always ridiculously and disproportionately grateful for the relatively small amount of planning necessary to orchestrate such events but even though Rupert knew that, the praise inflated his ego.

One of Rupert's event planning responsibilities was to procure the alcohol and since they had moved to the Square, he had been responsible for the wine cellar. Hugo was ridiculously afraid of small spaces which seemed very odd to Rupert but also fortuitous as it meant he had an extra personal domain. He kept it well stocked throughout the year so that when it came to these evenings he was prepared but nevertheless he had ordered an extra fifty bottles of Dom Perignon to be absolutely sure. It had almost certainly been unnecessary but it was better to have too many rather than too few and they would save.

It was his wont to delegate the catering and decoration to the outside caterers but he ensured that he presented them, in good time, with a precise plan and layout and insisted that it be accurately adhered to. He would, of course, build and serve from the champagne tower himself; it had become his piece de resistance and he could never trust anyone with such an important part of the evening. It was worth the painstaking effort because Hugo and his guests always seemed to appreciate it so highly. The caterers were bringing no less than three large chocolate fountains; one milk, one plain and one white as well as an old fashioned sweet cart. From previous experience he was sure that the 'children', which is how he thought of the silly, noisy rabble, would enjoy skewering as well as choosing their fruit, marshmallows and such like. For someone who didn't enjoy or attend parties by choice, he felt he had researched and organised this one rather well and possibly even better than usual. He thought that he may have surpassed himself by arranging for a vintage store to bring a fancy dress photo booth so that the children could dress up in silly costumes and accessories and then take home photographic evidence of their 'hilarious' antics. He groaned.

. . . .

Hugo sipped his tea appreciatively and smiled at the man he had known since childhood. The chap really was a wonder; he did everything utterly perfectly and was now unreservedly indispensible. Hugo really didn't know what he would do without him despite his funny ways and his being infuriatingly old fashioned, pompous and precise to the point of obsessive. Somehow the portentousness and pomposity added to his charm and was a small price to pay for his usefulness.

He had first proved himself to be invaluable at university when it had been evident that Hugo was far less academically bright than he. The now employer had struggled rather to complete his degree whilst coping with the rental of the three properties his mother and father had paid the deposits on, so that he would have an income whilst studying. His parents would never have been unkind or unconstructive enough to show their disappointment at him not having inherited the family brains and going to Oxford; they had tried to make the best of the situation by starting off his portfolio.

Whilst neither an entrepreneur nor a risk taker, Rupert had been easily and expertly able to balance his workload, follow instructions to the letter and be relied upon to act on his own initiative in day to day matters. Being the most adept in his year at computing, his methodical, analytical and logical mind allowed him to manage Hugo's portfolio, insurance, accounts and tax returns whist himself easily achieving a first. Hugo, in lieu of disbursement, had allowed him to stay rent free in one of the houses he owned. The following and final year, by mutual consent, he had moved Rupert into the house in which he resided so that they could more easily work. His employee had fortunately also shown himself to be discreet as Hugo had decided it was much more appropriate not to share the knowledge of his owner status with the other students and especially his tenants.

Sara had tip toed into Professor Thompson's lecture thirteen minutes late. She'd hoped to slip in unnoticed but that damn man saw everything; she could swear he had a sixth sense. He had looked up from the complex equation he was scribbling on the white board at the precise moment she'd slid into her seat and had raised his bushy eyebrows perceptively before continuing the narration of his maths. Whilst she had lost most of her enthusiasm for chemistry, she still retained the upmost respect and even affection for the Prof and felt a massive pang of guilt at disappointing him. As for the other students, who looked up disdainfully as she made what she decided to reframe as her fashionably late appearance; they could all go to hell. She was aware that she wasn't liked much, it wasn't particularly well hidden but it no longer hurt her and she thought it likely that they were probably just envious. It no doubt irked them that she always attained such good grades when she obviously cared so little about studying. It can't have helped their disapproval that the Prof not only never got impatient or reproachful of her flagrant lack of respect for his lectures but also often gave her extra privileges; so impressed was he by her gift.

. . . .

Blinking in the dazzling winter sunlight as she emerged from the not quite bright enough lecture theatre, Sara considered her immediate future. This had been her only study commitment of the day and had she known it would only cover the polymers with which she was already very familiar she would have stayed in bed! Now that she was up and about, however, a wander round the shops surely wouldn't go amiss. She brightened as she remembered that she needed to look for a pair of shoes to go with the beautiful shimmery dress that Hugo had bought her for his party. It was less than two weeks away so there was no time to lose; his parties were legendary and she could hardly wait! She could easily have walked or certainly caught a bus into town but neither of those were her style so she called three taxi firms till she found one who said they could be on campus quickly enough for her.

She thought it unlikely she would find anything suitable in the Princesshay shopping precinct and, after a cursory look round, her assumption was confirmed. The dress was exquisitely delicate and the shoe boots and platforms so in vogue and featured in all the shop windows were much too heavy. A little thrill of pleasure ran through her as she could now feel entirely justified resorting to her favourite but oh-so-expensive little boutique on Gandy Street. With a renewed spring in her step, she quickened her pace toward her spiritual home! She already had more shoes than anyone else she knew but she was always able to defend the decision to purchase a new pair, if only to lift her spirits; to Sara, shoes were the stuff of life.

....

Just ten minutes after she had been warmly welcomed by the ingratiating young sales assistant, she was looking down blissfully at her delightfully clad feet; the ivory skyscraper-high stiletto, peep-toe strapped courts were so perfect that she didn't even look at the price label. Three hundred and sixty-five pounds would probably be considered a more than ridiculous indulgence by the stuffy, plain chemists she had left on campus but Sara didn't even flinch as she passed over her American Express card. She was very aware that the shiny gold card that her super boyfriend had given her attracted more than a little attention from sales staff and it made her smile smugly to herself. She was a very lucky girl; Hugo was a great catch!

She thoroughly enjoyed carrying her designer carrier bag through the streets of Exeter; she knew she should feel guilty and maybe it made her a bad person but she couldn't help but take great pleasure in being ostentatious, in showing the world she had money. She had heard that some people felt nauseous when spending large amounts of money but she had never understood that. It always made her feel like a child with a new toy and today was no exception; she carried the bag containing her shoes like a badge. The majority of people who passed her wouldn't even recognise the boutique's name on the carrier, wouldn't appreciate anything her favourite shop sold anyway so they didn't matter. It was those who were familiar with the exclusive shop, those who couldn't quite afford it that she wanted to impress, whose admiration she craved.

Sara adored being able to spend money; it was still a huge novelty. Since her age had been in double figures there had been no money available at all. She'd worn hand me downs since forever and had suffered the taunts of children in neighbouring houses and been the butt of jokes at school. She'd hated never being able to follow fashion trends, always having to wear someone else's cast-off scuffed shoes and wearing coats with sleeves that were way too long or short. As a child, she could remember her family being reasonably, even comfortably, well off, having many of the newest toys and clothes and living in a large semi-detached house on the outskirts of Chester. She had loved her early childhood and had extremely fond memories of many visits to what she still believed was the best zoo in the world.

Sara's parents, Elizabeth and David Brampton had all but, - extremely regretfully- given up desperately trying for a baby when suddenly at forty-one her mother had fallen pregnant. Whilst she had counted her blessings every single day she'd carried her much hoped for baby, it had not been an easy pregnancy or, indeed, labour; of the symptoms she had suffered, the fainting, shortness of breath and swollen ankles had probably been the most debilitating. Sara's actual birth had been, without doubt, the highest point of Elizabeth's life and she had been overjoyed to have produced a perfect little girl but sadly, she herself had been left with permanent and incapacitating heart problems.

David, eleven years his wife's senior was now seventy-three and suffered from multiple health conditions including diabetes for which he was insulin dependent. Sara hardly recognised the ailing, grey, old husks as the loving, gentle people who had done everything possible to be the parents they believed their little girl deserved. As Sara had grown out of toddlerhood and into an infant, it had quickly transpired, to her doting parents' delight that their long awaited only child was exceptionally bright. Her junior school had entered her into a 'gifted and talented' program and given her many opportunities to learn further. For their part, in order to allow her to reach her full potential, Elizabeth and David had scrimped and saved to send her to a private school when she reached eleven.

Sara ardently wished they had not; had allowed her a normal life - with fashionable clothes. The bullying she had endured for having parents the age of other people's grandparents had been difficult enough but the shame of associating with children who had so very much when she had had so very little, paled it into insignificance. One would have hoped that the young ladies at her expensive school would have been more tolerant and less judgmental than their less educated contemporaries but this, she had discovered the hard way, was not the case. But now, strutting along with new shoes paid for by a boyfriend who was even richer than most of their families she felt free and a million miles away from their cruel mocking; she felt entirely justified in making up for all her years of deprivation and discomfort. After all, Hugo loved her and took great pleasure in seeing her wearing the beautiful clothes that he could afford without difficulty. He was her freedom, her meal ticket, her gold mine, yes, but she wasn't the heartless, opportunist parasite that it could be assumed; she actually loved him very, very much.

Chapter Two

Hugo was supposed to be working. He knew he was supposed to be working. He wasn't working. He was sitting at the beautiful, antique oak desk with its gilded green leather inlay that his parents had bought him for his twenty-first birthday three years ago, with his chin in his hands, daydreaming about Sara and the weekend they'd just spent together. She really was the most incredible girl he'd ever met and the eighteen months they'd been together had been the happiest of his whole life. A familiar warm glow of pride flowed through him as he remembered how it had felt to see people's appreciative glances toward her whenever they went out together.

At the theatre recently, an elderly lady had actually come across to tell him how lucky he was to have such a rare beauty of a lady on his arm. Her delicate, petite, willowy frame, her intense grey eyes, her fine, long, white blond hair and almost translucent porcelain skin gave her the ephemeral look of a fairy. Of an angel. She was breath taking and it was a constant source of delight to him knowing he wasn't the only one to see it. She was his fragile, perfect princess and he tried his best to be her handsome prince or at least her knight in shining armour! He loved nothing more than being able to care for her in any way he could. Whilst he liked to see her as vulnerable and fragile, he also appreciated that she had an exceedingly fine mind and a very strong will. She was extraordinarily intelligent. (Why was everyone so much cleverer than he?) Yet when they were together they each managed to employ and enjoy the roles of protector and protected. Their symbiotic relationship worked well for both of them and they found it harder and harder, each week, to spend time apart. Without her, he felt as if he were only half there, as if half of him were missing, leaving him a shell, a shadow and already he yearned to see her again, to become whole.

He roused himself from these cheerless musings and allowed his mind to leap forward to their party the weekend after next. He loved parties and especially loved throwing his own. He could act 'mine host' really well but admitted that he didn't actually do anything toward them, except for giving Rupert a guest list to invite and a free range with his credit card. It always amazed him that his assistant could organise such a good event when he didn't even like them himself! Yet he knew he could completely trust him to put on a bloody good evening.

Hugo was most excited about showing Sara off to all of his friends, of course. She was going to wear the dress he'd just bought her. If it were possible for her to look even more beautiful than usual, then she did so in the delicate silvery dress that suited her exquisitely. He'd *had* to buy it for her; he'd loved buying it for her! He enjoyed spending money on her at least as much as she loved receiving presents. He lived to see her thrilled little face when she opened gifts or had things paid for her. He also loved to see her in the clothes and jewellery he'd bought or chosen for her; he felt that it strengthened and enhanced his position as her boyfriend. As much as he was thoroughly enjoying that role, he looked forward to being able, in the not too distant future, to promote himself to fiancé and then to husband. All he had to do was choose the right ring, obtain her father's permission and pluck up the courage to ask her! His mind planned excitedly; as soon as they were married, they could get a dog, or two. He knew that Sara loved dogs, particularly Labradors and especially chocolate brown ones. Maybe they could be her wedding present from him? He'd been brought up surrounded by golden retrievers and spaniels and would love to have animals again. He could hardly wait to have Sara as his wife and to start a family with her when she was ready; she would make the most beautiful babies in the world!

Hugo turned on his laptop and expertly managing to sidestep the portfolio folder that he should be working on and Googled 'cute Labrador puppy' images. He chose a sweet chocolate brown one that was snuggled up in a cosy Christmas fleece and WhatsApped it to Sara along with eight kisses and then rocked back in his chair, satisfied. Almost immediately she replied

'Awww....I'm such a lucky girl to have you. Love you always xxxxxxxxxxxxxxxxxxxxxxxx'

He was definitely the lucky one! The banner floating across his Mac screen alerted him momentarily to a list of possible new rental properties. He stretched luxuriantly, yawned and settled back to his reverie. He knew Sara was materialistic and sometimes even a little immodest but why shouldn't she be when she'd had such difficult and traumatising teenage years? She deserved every last luxury he could provide for her. He relished the challenge of making her feel totally secure. Of helping her feel it was normal and natural that she should receive gifts from him and possess pretty things. In truth, if he could have had his way, he would wrap her up in a cashmere blanket and keep her safe and comfortable and happy forever. He also knew that he *really* should be working! He couldn't justify any further procrastination so, reluctantly, he returned his awareness to prospective investments.

....

Rupert knew that his master very rarely achieved anything on Mondays and he had long since given up making appointments for him at the very beginning of the week. He was extremely fond of his benefactor but, if he were honest, Hugo probably would never get an awful lot done at all if it were not for him; and he didn't mind at all. Hugo was a kind, philanthropic and steady sort of chap and had given him a raison d'être when Rupert had first escaped to Bristol. For this he owed him a debt of gratitude and in any case, his employer's business wasn't exactly difficult or high risk; Rupert could have run it in his sleep. Essentially, all that had to be done was to identify good investments, buy and sell at the right time, manage them and do the books; not exactly rocket science. Whilst Hugo often floundered under stress, Rupert found it effortless to make decisions quickly, multi tasked with ease and wasn't afraid of hard work. He felt utterly loyal to Hugo and considered himself extremely lucky to receive such a generous salary and accommodation in a beautiful suite in Hugo's home for completing tasks he found very undemanding. If he had any concerns at all about his perfect job, it

13

was that there wasn't always enough work to keep him busy but he knew that would improve as the business grew even further. He considered this temporary tedium a very small price to pay. He rose early each day, often before it was light and as he liked to keep himself occupied, before the agents and auctioneers had started uploading onto the net, this morning, he had cleaned his living quarters from top to bottom; twice.

As a student, Rupert had always, of course, kept his own accommodation impeccably, partly out of respect for Hugo but also because it would have been unthinkable for him not to keep his and all the public areas of a residence in which he resided at a standard he felt satisfactory. He had found that he could never settle comfortably in a house that wasn't completely ordered, both in areas that could be seen and those that could not. It was not unusual for him to clean inside not only his clothes drawers and wardrobes but also inside the kitchen cupboards, oven and fridge more than once a day if he deemed or believed that they had become contaminated in any way.

The housekeeper that Hugo had employed, in his opinion, was worse than useless and could not be relied upon to do anything other than the most menial of tasks and was certainly not welcome in his rooms. He wished he had jurisdiction over the staff; he would organise the 'help' very differently and it wouldn't just fill out his time somewhat and provide the household with more efficient cleaners and cooks but also and maybe most essentially, to him, being a man-manager would make him feel important.

He would arrange a workforce commensurate to a house the size of theirs. Rather than opting to employ a separate cook and cleaner, Hugo just had a live in housekeeper, the widowed Mrs Cappott and a part time gardener they used during the summer months. His master had reasoned that she could have her finger on the pulse of everything and also be there when he went on holiday. Rupert disliked people sharing any part of his and Hugo's living space, knew that he personally could look after the house on the rare occasions that Hugo travelled and particularly didn't like the idea of keeping all ones eggs in the same basket. It was too much of a worry that the sole member of staff would get sick or leave; these people had no loyalty or respect.

Rupert managed to work round having such a sub standard housekeeper by overseeing all the damn woman's tasks and when necessary, completing those tasks himself. Irritatingly, whilst Hugo appeared to have enjoyed the interviewing and recruiting of his employees, Rupert felt his judgement, except of course in his own case, suspect in this matter. Worse still, kindly Hugo didn't enjoy disciplining or dismissing staff so the household was forever cursed with the very unsatisfactory and lazy old Mrs Cappott.

Since the very first time she had supposedly cleaned his room, after which, on inspection, he had discovered smears on his shaving mirror and crumbs still in the tray under his toaster, he had never let the incompetent woman back into his rooms. As a necessary precaution he had also removed his keys from her set so that she couldn't be tempted to re enter; he didn't want the old bat snooping.

Once satisfied with the perfect orderliness of his compact but beautiful apartment, he had checked the market for all new and relevant properties and made appointments to see any worth looking at. He knew that the master was very unlikely to feel the need to view them internally but Rupert liked to see, if only for completeness, all the interiors. These houses were only for renting to undiscerning and, more often than not, disgusting students and young sharers. They had to be merely adequate but he would feel lacking in his duties if he wasn't thorough.

The great majority of the 257 tenants in the 63 properties Hugo owned lived like pigs; he wrinkled his nose as if he had smelt something nasty and wondered, not for the first time, if he could persuade Hugo to add a range of houses for more discriminating renters to his portfolio. Fortunately Rupert's duties didn't include interviewing the tenants or visiting the properties once the contracts had been signed; he merely had to appoint managing agents who liaised between the various renters and maintenance contractors.

Nevertheless, arranging the procurement of a better class of property would, for him, feel more rewarding.

. . . .

It had been such an enormous relief to have a space to call his own after living for so long with *her*. He simultaneously screwed up his nose and twisted his lips as he recalled that grim period of his life. To himself, he always referred to Aunt Joanne simply and derogatorily as 'her'. Not that he thought of her or his time with her very often at all. After the incident of what she had called his parents' 'dreadful demise', he, then an orphan and a minor, had been sent to live with her, his mother's older and only sister in a God forsaken part of southwest Scotland. Demonstrably but inexplicably to him, many people actually chose both to live and visit there.

Almost overnight he had been removed from everything and everyone he knew and been cruelly deposited into an existence that couldn't have been more different to the life he was used to. He had only met her previously on a small handful of occasions and knew her not at all. She was as thrilled to suddenly have the teenage son of a sibling she hadn't even particularly liked in her home as he was to be there. For five long years, they had both done their upmost to avoid any contact with each other; they had been two strangers sharing the same small space, ignoring one another as if each had existed in separate dimensions.

Eventually he had got to know their tiny hamlet and desolate surroundings and comprehend the accent well enough to understand just how much he was being bullied but had never made any acquaintances, let alone friends. Much of his time was taken up at the nearest educational institution for his age. The almost intolerable seven and a half hour day was lengthened further by two half hour nightmarish school bus rides. He had spent his non school time studying alone in his miniscule room in which one could not have swung the proverbial feline.

The summer months were easier; to keep himself from going insane with boredom he had developed a routine; on all evenings when there was enough light, he would arrive back to the cottage, he couldn't bring himself to call it home, complete his homework and then fully check the tiny rooms for anything amiss before heading out with the shotgun he had found in the little shed. He had never really known exactly what he had meant and still meant by 'amiss', he just knew that he couldn't go out before he had checked. The size of his room in those days had made this a much less time consuming task than it was today but there were still drawers and wardrobes and, of course, under the bed to search. He'd never really questioned the time it took to complete these checks, any more than he begrudged the length of time it took to, say, clean his teeth. Even on bad days when he had to verify his safety on multiple occasions, he had just accepted that this was just the way it was to feel protected. He had never found anything in all of his searches but felt the undefined horror of the possibility of some kind of evil lurking, until he had investigated every possible hiding place.

He had painstakingly taught himself to shoot rabbits for fun. The physical task had not come as easily as studying and until he had perfected his aim, many a hapless rabbit had been maimed and wounded. It entertained him to muse that the rabbits were actually no more damaged than a cat would have been had he had one with which to confirm the size of his room!

Leaving the generic two up, two down and the village that had incarcerated him for sixty protracted months, 260 weeks, 1826 days, 43,824 hours, 2,629,440 minutes, 157,766,400 seconds had been a tremendous liberation. He smiled to himself; enjoying the mathematics. The halls in which he had spent his first year at Bristol had felt luxurious enough after feeling imprisoned for so long but moving to Hugo's large Victorian shared house had been like heaven. His family home had been of a good average size but had not had the five bedrooms his landlord's had or showcased the plethora of attractive original features. Often when the other students were out, he had walked through all their rooms imagining that the whole house were his, taking pleasure from the space around him and the comparative opulence; the horrible messiness of the rooms over which he had no control was the only thing that had marred his dream. Occasionally, here at Redcliffe Square, without the mess and with much more grandeur, he still made believe that he were the lord of the manor, the master himself!

Rupert glanced into Hugo's study and saw the same glazed expression that his master had exhibited all morning. It amused the PA that his employer even bothered to sit at his great Nellie of a desk when both of them knew he wasn't going to actually work. Rupert had always completed the work Hugo imagined he was doing before Hugo even switched on his Apple Mac. He would never, though, be so unkind or disrespectful as to let his employer know that he'd already done the work.

Gaining no acknowledgement he backed quietly into the hallway and as he did so, caught sight of himself in the tall, ornate gilt mirror. He was, as always, smart and tidily dressed in slacks, shirt, tie and plain woollen waistcoat. He moved forward a little, enlarging his reflection and tweaked his moustache. No one kept a good moustache these days which was a great pity in his opinion as he believed that grooming was tremendously important. Each morning he made sure that he washed and shaved very carefully and slicked back his dark hair before carefully dressing in clothes that he had pressed the previous evening; he always preferred to over rather than under dress. Satisfied with the neatness of his appearance, he strode silently and purposefully back to his rooms. His posture and gait were impeccable and his walking style was as controlled and as measured as everything else in his life.

Chapter Three

Hugo's stomach growled, reminding him it was nearly lunch time and how ravenous he was. He always dined out more than usual at the weekend and his body still expected the same amount of sustenance on a Monday. To give himself a semblance of achievement, he quickly glanced through the properties that had come on the market today that fitted his criteria and printed off a short list of those he could be interested in. After a slow start the morning had actually flowed quite well really and he was pleased with his success at seeing a couple of definite possibilities.

He was already completely out of work mode, seconds later, as he absentmindedly dropped the print out into Rupert's tray and was looking forward to his regular lunch appointment with his financial advisor and now friend, Jonathan. They had initiated this habit several years previously when Jonathan had begun organising Hugo's loans and other financial interests and it had quickly become a regular weekly event which was enjoyed by both men.

Hugo collected his warm sheepskin hat and new camel coat from the hat stand in the corner of the room. He checked his gloves were in the coat pockets, glanced out of the sash window to ascertain that it was not raining, called a half hearted goodbye to Rupert and set off. He travelled along the tree-lined square with its grassed common, on foot, to the nearby bistro which had been favoured and frequented by local business men for two and a half decades.

Within no time he was entering the green canopied La Bouchee, the lovely little boutique restaurant that served the best French food he'd tasted outside France. He could see that his good friend was already sitting at what had become 'their' table. This place was like coming home; he breathed in the wonderful and familiar aroma and sighed contentedly. He loved the flicker and the smell of the candles and the eclectic mix of antiques and felt his body and mind relaxing as he slid into his usual seat.

"Jonathan" he beamed as his friend stood to welcome him. Hugo pushed his gloves into his pockets and shook his friend's hand before they both took their places. This formal greeting still continued from their early meetings in this very establishment and had become a tradition they both now found amusing. Before Hugo had even settled into his seat, the seemingly ubiquitous and wonderful waiter, Jacques had relieved him of his hat and coat, hung them safely and returned with the menus and specials, two glasses and a jug of chilled, iced water.

"Lovely to see you gentlemen" he smiled, as he poured the water, ever the dutiful waiter. "I'll be back shortly to take your food order. Any drinks in the meantime? Your usuals..?" He hesitated because, depending on Jonathan's diet of the moment, his 'usual' altered fairly drastically. With an "I'm fine with the water thank you" from his inconsistent regular and a dependable "White wine, please, your driest" Jacques turned towards the bar returning what only seemed like seconds later with Hugo's wine. The sight of Jacques' approaching figure caused them both to quickly scan the specials chalk board and knowing the menu so well, be ready and able to order by the time the waiter reached their fashionable worn and rustic table.

"You're back on the wagon then?" enquired Hugo, sipping from what would be his only glass.

"Yes *and* calorie counting." Jonathan groaned resignedly, patting his small paunch. He was several inches taller than Hugo but still too padded for his height.

"I know I'm only two years older than you but I think it's middle age spread" he grinned.

"It's much easier this time though, Jane, the marvel is helping me."

Jane was the hypnotherapist that Jonathan had used to successfully combat his fear of flying. It had been life changing for him and to this marvel, he was eternally grateful. He recommended her to everyone with any problem a hypnotherapist could feasibly help with.

"I hope it won't spoil our party for you? You are still coming? You've got eleven days to cut enough calories to have a blowout"

"Of course, old chap, I wouldn't miss one of your parties for the world. I keep thinking I might meet the woman of my dreams at one....but I'm still waiting!"

"Maybe this will be the one! Still on for tonight?" said the taller man.

Mondays and Thursdays were run nights and they always ran the same five mile route; another tradition that defined and cemented their relationship.

"Of course" rejoined Hugo, sipping his water. "Shall we try and beat forty-five minutes?"

A running joke, in more ways than one. The course had taken three quarters of an hour every time they had run it, twice a week, for over a year.

"Forty-four and a half?" ventured a laughing Jonathan as their food arrived.

....

Rupert picked up the untidily abandoned print-out that Hugo had left for him, gave it a cursory glance to confirm there was nothing he hadn't himself seen and placed it, tidily folded, on his recycling pile. He smiled affectionately as he thought of his master preparing and no doubt being proud of the redundant list. He sighed contentedly as he looked around the study. He enjoyed Monday lunchtimes. It was one of the few times during the week that he had the whole house to himself, all five storeys of it, yet could also look forward to the Master's fairly imminent return.

He closed his eyes and breathed in the tranquillity, the beauty and the majesty, the century and a half of elegance. During these quiet times, to all intents and purposes this magnificent building was his. Although only an employee it was his home and he felt swollen with pride.

21

This veritable mansion was a world away from the single room within the miniscule hovel in which he had endured his teenage years. He very rarely allowed his thoughts to stray into life before that time and, of course, the university halls had been very transitory; his present abode was the only place he had ever thought of as home.

His favourite part of the house was the dining room; it was beautiful as well as functional and because it was used only on special occasions, as they usually ate in the breakfast room, it had a peaceful, opulent feel to it. He walked into the light, airy, spacious room and appreciated the grandeur that encapsulated everything superior and luxurious about his new lifestyle. Hugo had hired an interior designer when they first moved to London; whilst having no skills in that department himself he had wanted to live in an attractively furnished and decorated house. The designer had come armed with boards of ideas, swatches of materials and samples of paint. Rupert had been consulted about the dining room when Hugo had reached his fill of decor and had felt ridiculously important choosing the natural and simple hues he now observed.

He ran his fingers along the grain of the huge yew dining table and took pleasure in the smoothness, the solidity, the immortality encased within the varnish. He drew out one of the twelve claw footed dining chairs and seated on its ivory jacquard brocade upholstery was the master of all he surveyed. His eyes slid over the matching sideboard with its silk-tassled keys, the fine paintings and the long drapes that puddled onto the parquet floor. The highly polished herringbone wooden flooring flowed through all the reception rooms as did the glossed white deep skirting boards and the panelled doors. He scanned the plasterwork coving and ceiling roses and the ornate fireplace which was rarely lit and currently filled with enormous pine cones.

Food as well as accommodation came with his employment and having simple tastes he was able to save practically all his wages. It wouldn't be too long before he could afford the deposit on his own home but what would be the point in his owning a property? It would be merely an empty and soulless box. It was the fact that this house was Hugo's, a man he respected that made it feel right. It was that and the additional benefit of it feeling so much like his own that gratified him. Rupert was aware that he didn't 'do' emotion like other people but he liked Hugo more than he had liked anybody. Comparing his fondness, if that was what it was, for Hugo with that for other people he had known, provoked a rare reminiscence.

He had not been able to trust his mother. She had often been too irrational, too forgetful and too unpredictable. He had grown up not being able to depend on her being there physically, emotionally or mentally. Though there had been times, occasionally lasting for as long as several weeks or even months when she was a sweet and loving mother, he had learned that these short happinesses were only temporary. They were not to be depended or relied upon not to disappear without notice.

He reluctantly remembered that as a tiny infant looking through the gaps in his shielding fingers, seeing her screaming and thrashing about uncontrollably. He had watched her crouching...rocking ...whimpering...whispering....wholly unaware of his presence, let alone his needs. He had regularly lain alone, hungry and frightened when his father was out at work and his mother was God knew where physically and the devil knew where mentally. She'd often hissed, howled or sobbed at him that the hopelessness and despair that had led to the alcoholism which held her tightly in its grasp had stemmed from the post natal depression she had suffered after giving birth to him, her only child. The depression that he had caused. The addiction that he had caused. The insanity that he had caused. She believed that she was what she was because of him; that the relentless and overpowering pull of volatility, of imbalance, of weakness was his fault. She had told him over and over that she'd thought having a child would be a wonderful, spiritual experience but that it had been an unvarying living hell and she hated him for that. He in turn had hated and been terrified by the quicksand of her moods, the slipperiness of her grip on reality, the plethora of forgotten promises and the disappointments.

His father, he had been able to trust. The strong and wise man had kept his wife out of institutions and been his son's constant, his brick, his stability, the centre of his world. Rupert had wanted his mother to be taken away, had yearned to feel safe and secure without her fear-provoking presence but his caring father had not been able to bring himself to abandon the sane woman he wanted to hope was cowering somewhere inside what she had become. His father had told him often that she had been a lovely, sensible young woman when they had first met and he still optimistically anticipated that he'd get his wife back.

In their early married life, she had been easily able to work full time as a receptionist for a busy engineering firm and keep their home impeccably. When she had fallen pregnant ten months after they had wed, they had decided, as a couple that she should be a stay at home mother. Unhappily she hadn't even been able to perform her motherly duties reliably and Gregory had essentially lost his wife and the tender relationship they had shared. He missed them both terribly and he hadn't been about to turn his back on her in this time of need; he had made vows about sickness and health and better and worse and he had intended to stand by them. Rupert had learned to cope. Learned to shut her and her madness out. He had learned not to be lulled into a false sense of security by any periods of normality, not to allow himself the pain of the recurrent realisation that they always ended and gave way to the anarchy of his mother's usual existence.

He experienced his mother's passing as a relief as well as a welcome opportunity to spend more time with the now free long suffering widower. To his horror, shock and disbelief, it hadn't worked out like that. The adolescent Rupert had been incredulous and rocked to his very core when his father had not only taken the loss desperately badly but, inexplicably could no longer even look at his son. In his darkest times, those averted eyes still haunted him. His mother, though no longer with them, apparently still had an insidious grip of power over the poor man.

He shook himself; he didn't like to think of all the details, of all the cruel twists and blows fate had dealt but suffice to say that late one spring evening only days after her death, the shell of his beloved father had walked, Reginald Perrin like, into the sea. Unlike the fictional character he had never returned. Despite himself, despite the intense love he'd had for him, Rupert had viewed being left an orphan, as the ultimate betrayal. He deplored all weakness, had loathed it in his mother, refused now to tolerate it in others and *never* sanctioned it in himself.

Confusion and pain had reigned for the next lonely handful of years until Hugo had become his saviour. Though not as wise as his father, Hugo was continually dependable, steady..safe.

Chapter Four

Sara sipped her skinny latte and nibbled blissfully on her chocolate dreamcake Krispy Kreme doughnut. Today was the treat day she allowed herself every three weeks to keep herself sane and kick start her metabolism. The rule she'd decided on was that she still had to record all the calories, making sure that eating was a conscious activity and she must not exceed eighteen hundred kcal - which was well over double what she allowed herself on normal days. Doughnuts were one of her favourite indulgences and these were her doughnuts of choice. It was unbelievably delicious and she made sure that she ate it mindfully, concentrating on every flavour and texture so as to fully value it. Once she had finished she licked her delicate fingers and added the 389 kilocalories to the very indulgent 110kcal she had eaten for breakfast and entered the day's running total on to the 'calories' column on her phone's note page.

As well as calories consumed the document also contained the date and her naked weight when she first got out of bed. Fortunately these days more and more cafes and restaurants displayed the energy their produce contained and if they didn't, she could search it on Google. She was also very practised and accurate at estimating and she didn't eat *anything* she couldn't record. Treat days were fabulous because this evening wouldn't have to be tough. Normally this amount of calories at this time of day would have necessitated a *very light* dinner, no supper and a sleepless and hungry night. She was going to make the most of today because the next eleven days would have to be very lean; she didn't intend to do anything to jeopardise fitting into her new dress. She discussed her way of maintaining her weight with no one but even this secretiveness didn't cause her to consider herself to have the eating disorder her friends and housemates accused her of. She did recognise that her relationship with food was rather unhealthy, but then, whose wasn't? She couldn't think of any slim woman who wasn't exactly the same as she and anyone who pretended otherwise was lying.

One couldn't live in today's society of celebrity diets and air brushed models, be the necessary size 6-8 and be healthy! It amused her to know that dear Hugo thought she was naturally tiny. Weekends, the time she spent with him, were hard for her because he liked to eat out so much. She knew that buying her expensive meals was one of the ways he showed her love and was easily hurt by her rejection of it but it meant that she had to practically starve herself for the rest of the week to keep her daily average at the right level. She was clever at pretending she'd already eaten on Fridays before she met him and that she would eat on Sunday nights with friends at home. Sometimes she had to resort to the old bulimia trick on Saturdays or at the very least, a long 'healthy and fun' run before breakfast. She wasn't overly concerned about her vomiting because it was rarely more than once a week and hopefully she'd think of something more sustainable before she moved in with Hugo full time. She couldn't realistically fit any more gym sessions into her week but there was always lipo!

The control she exhibited over her eating hadn't actually ever been anything to do with her weight in the beginning. It had just been a method of self control and originally a way of controlling her parents. Whenever she had felt she was losing management of the way she wanted to live she could at least be in charge of what she ingested. It was a way she coped in a world she sometimes felt her grasp of which was slipping through her fingers. It was her own little rock, something to hold onto, a safe island in her perceived shifting sea of chaos. The less of a grip she had on the way she could dress, the way people treated her and her relationships, the more she sought solace in the power she yielded over her body. She didn't feel that she was doing anything different from the majority of women. It worked for her, it always had; it had suited her well and was a friend she wasn't interested in losing, a life partner she loyally and jealously guarded.

. . . .

Happily full of escargot and coq au vin, Hugo placed his cutlery onto his plate and dropped the napkin on top of it. Both men sat back into their chairs, satiated.

"So, any new properties you need mortgages for?" Jonathan beamed at his friend who was now single-handedly responsible for a whole third of Jonathan's work and in referrals for a further third. It was because of Hugo that Jonathan had dared leave his job at a large financial firm and gone it alone. Becoming self employed when he had his own mortgage to pay had been scary but he was mightily pleased that he had because his earnings had increased exponentially. Being his own boss and choosing his hours satisfied him very well indeed.

"No, but there will be shortly, I had an offer accepted on a six bedroomed HMO yesterday. Do you need me to sign the remortgages you were doing? Oh..and has Rupert sorted out the insurances?" As he asked he knew there was no need to check about the cover. Of course Rupert would have sorted it; he had never once let him down.

"Yes, old man, insurances on both the London and Bristol properties are all up to date, of course, no need to worry. I think I can save you a bit of dosh on the re-mortgages; I'm looking at more competitive group policies. So what's the new 'house of multiple occupation' like?" he enunciated the full title pedantically.

"Have you actually looked at this one?!" Jonathan teased, knowing it was most unlikely his friend would have set foot in the proposed addition to his portfolio but that good old Rupert would have gone in, unbidden, to check its suitability. Jonathan was extremely pleased that his friend had an assistant he felt he coultrust and think so highly of and he was well aware of the man's dependability but his eccentricities day in day out would have driven him crazy. He must be much less intolerant than Hugo because Rupert's obsessive attention to detail and prissiness would preclude him being able to work any more closely with him than he already had to; the conversations they had to share as it was were already more than enough.

"It was only for renting" carefree Hugo answered "and Rupert likes to do it. If the valuation is enough for the buy to let mortgage lender and it's been renting happily for several years then it's good enough for me. Why would I need to see it?"

"I see your point, my friend, but you didn't even look round the whole *five* stories of your own home!!" Another joke between the two. Jonathan considered himself to be well and truly blessed that he could have such a good relationship with the person responsible for tripling his income.

"I didn't need to...." Hugo paused before they both finished off

"Rupert checked it" and the pair dissolved into fits of laughter, more akin to school boys' behaviour to that of successful business men. Once they had regained control Jonathan offered

"Seriously, the Marvel Jane could easily sort you out, she's an absolute wonder with hypnotherapy. She'll have you feeling happy in tiny lifts, never mind your own bloody wine cellar. You should call her, what have you got to lose? Don't you agree that it's a tiny bit odd you haven't seen part of your own home? I don't know why you don't give her a go, she's helped so many of my friends and flying was a complete nightmare for me before she took away my fear. I tell you, the woman's a marvel!"

Hugo knew he really should do something about the claustrophobia which encumbered his life quite frequently but he just wasn't ready to face it yet. He could cope with it, just about, and the thought of having to confront it head on was too daunting. He didn't really understand hypnotherapy and wasn't at all sure he wanted anybody, even the 'marvel' Jane messing about in his head. He felt silly enough having to make excuses not to go into lifts and other confined spaces without having to bare his soul and admit his fears in front of a stranger. He didn't have a clue what happened when you were in trance or whatever they did to you. What if she found something embarrassing? What if he said something stupid?

He suddenly became aware that Jonathan was looking at him expectantly.

"One day I'll call her...maybe "he said doubtfully "and meanwhile...I don't need to go down into my cellar..." and together they chorused

"I've got Rupert!"

Chapter Five

Hugo wrapped his cashmere camel coat more tightly around his chilled body, turned up the collar, pulled his hat a little further down over his ears and pushed his hands into his warm gloves. He didn't enjoy the inconvenience or the unpleasantness of the cold but he still loved this time of year; it felt cosy to be already dark at four in the afternoon and the tree lined avenue looked so festive twinkling with a thousand Christmas lights. He felt very contented with his world as he counted his many blessings and chuckled again about the jokes he had shared with his good friend. He always enjoyed Jonathan's company and considered himself to be very lucky to have such dependable people around him. There was only thing that troubled him very slightly and it was that Rupert and Sara weren't as close to each other as he would have liked but was sure they'd get on famously once they got to know one another better. He was well aware of Rupert's idiosyncrasies and the way he could appear pompous but he was a good chap and he hoped that Sara would soon appreciate how useful he was to have around. As for Rupert, he had no idea why anyone couldn't love Sara; she was completely perfect. He had always assumed, without judgement, that Rupert was gay which could maybe have explained it in part. Rupert had never shown any romantic or other interest in women and would be too old fashioned to admit an inclination toward men but then, when could he have had a relationship with either sex? He hardly ever left the house and received no guests. He didn't seem to need anybody. Maybe he was asexual; some people were, apparently. Maybe he was a misanthrope or simply overwhelmed by Sara's perfection.

Hugo was so deeply submerged in his thoughts that he nearly bumped straight into a little crowd of red wool clad, Redcliffe lower school mites. He cursed himself silently for being so distracted and apologised profusely. At least the group of older, still bright red clothed students were more in his eye line when, only a few seconds later he had already forgotten he should be concentrating thus alerting him to their presence and avoiding a clumsy collision. Returning immediately to his thoughts he conceded that Rupert was undoubtedly a little unusual but it was merely the type of thing one affectionately called foibles in somebody one liked and only oddness in someone one didn't.

The two men had first met when Rupert's late mother, Helen, had been newly employed to clean the Bradley-Smethurst family home in Christchurch, Dorset. Being the summer holidays he had been home from boarding school and as he remembered, was enjoying reconnecting with his home. He liked school and even though he was never one of the brighter students, to say the least, he had been good at sport and affable enough to have made copious friends. Nevertheless, he and certainly his mother would have preferred he had been a day boy at one of the two and a half dozen private Dorset schools but his father had been adamant about St. Paul's as the family's last few generations of boys had studied there.

It was funny to think he now lived only three miles from where he had spent most of his childhood. During one day of that particular summer vacation, Rupert had been brought along to work by his mother and had sat quietly in a corner listening to music through the earphones of his CD walkman. Hugo had been sent by his mother to see if the boy would like a glass of milk and a biscuit and that was how they had discovered a mutual obsession with Dido. Both adolescents had taken their drinks and digestives to Hugo's room to listen to more of her albums on Hugo's stereo and play chess. Only three weeks and cleaning visits later, their respective employee and mother had died, the poor woman's husband had taken his own life and Rupert had moved away. Hugo, always a sensitive boy, had felt very sorry for him despite not knowing him well and wished there had been something he could have done to help. He himself had such a close and happy family and gained a tremendous amount of strength and support from the tight unit; it had been unthinkable that poor Rupert was now practically alone. When, by chance, years later they attended the same university, it had been the least he felt he could do to help him out in any way he could. As it had turned out, God knew, he had profited at least as much from their affiliation.

It was a relief to be back in doors and he rubbed his still sheepskin clad hands together to help warm them up and smiled cheerfully. He was excited that Christmas was only seven weeks away; his family always had enormous Christmases and this would be the first one Sara had spent with him. Their relationship had been just a little too new ten months ago but this year was going to be very, very special.

The Bradley-Smethursts had always celebrated in the country house in which he'd been brought up on the South Coast, not at all far from Bournemouth. Though his parents only spent the minority of their time there now, it was big and convenient for guests to get to and stay in. As they spent a growing number of months in the gites that they had renovated in Southern France and their apartment in Venice, the house was mainly occupied by their housekeeper and her husband. Together the couple kept the house and garden spick and span throughout the year and always warm and ready for visits. He fondly looked forward to the roaring fires, the enormous decorated spruce they had in the drawing room each Christmas and particularly showing his sweetheart around the house and grounds where he had spent all of his early childhood. He had already bought her gift; a beautiful white and yellow gold bracelet he knew she'd love. She liked not being tied to one colour of gold so the bracelet with its seven delicate diamonds should be perfect and he couldn't wait to see her face when she opened it. On Boxing Day, Sara and he had arranged for to go to her parents' house in Cheshire. If they left at eight sharp after an early breakfast with no traffic at that time of year, a following wind and a bit of luck, they hoped to get there for the two o'clock lunch. It would be the first time Hugo had met them and he was a little nervous; he badly wanted to make the right impression as a sensible and trustworthy suitor.

Chapter Six

Sarah awoke and tried to roll over; she winced painfully. Her body ached all over, her throat felt raw and the sandpaper swallowing as she sipped the day old water hurt almost as much as the head thumping that had increased almost intolerably with the slight movement. She groaned and pulled the duvet up with difficulty, shivering yet perspiring enough to dampen her bedclothes. Why did this have to happen to her now? She was hardly ever ill and had been absolutely fine until she had needed to go to bed early with a headache last night. She was supposed to be going to Hugo's tomorrow, she missed him dreadfully and it was unthinkable to miss their weekend tradition; was there any chance she could stop herself feeling lousy by then? It wouldn't be a hard weekend after all, it wasn't the party yet, thank goodness, and she didn't need to drive because lovely Hugo always paid for first class train tickets and the taxi fare at both ends of the journey. So all she'd have to do was get there and then take it easy. She was already silly excited about the following weekend and wearing her new dress and shoes and wanted to show him them together before the party.

Not one to give in to illness lightly, she heaved herself up uncomfortably, her skin sore as the sheet scraped over it and forced herself to make a cup of tea and take two paracetamol. Feeling fragile and a little light headed she decided to go back to bed and rest for a while to give the tablets time to fix her.

....

She must have fallen asleep. The nerves in her legs felt like they were wired to the mains and the light bursting through the gap in her curtains burnt her eyes, causing her to see little sparks of gold floating round the room. She felt very peculiar indeed. Even though her body felt too tender she felt like she needed a cuddle. Maybe she should phone Hugo or her parents? Her phone was in her handbag at the foot of the bed, much too far away to easily reach. She wished that her arms could stretch out like Mr. Tickle's or that she could float over to it. She seemed to recall that she had been able to fly once as a child and wished she could remember how she'd done it. She wondered if she was remembering properly but before her rational mind could kick in she was following another fever induced fantasy about fairies getting the phone for her, charging it and calling someone for a hug and a hand out of bed. She thought of calling out to see if her housemates were in but it all seemed too difficult and too tiring and she didn't really care anyway. She knew that leaving her bed, let alone the house today was out of the question so there was no point wasting time and energy thinking about it. She closed her eyes and tried to ignore the drumming in her skull.

. . . .

Hugo had been beside himself and had felt physically sick when Sara hadn't phoned him this morning. She always called without fail. She was the later riser so he always left it to her so as not to disturb her beauty sleep but at 11.30am he had started to worry. She hadn't been at a party the night before so she should definitely have been up by then. He'd tried her phone, checked Twitter, Instagram and Facebook and turned his phone and computer off and on several times to check if there could have been a fault. He had tried to call Maggie and Lucy, Sara's housemates, but both phones had gone to voicemail. Where was she??

He paced as he replayed, over and over in his mind, every scene from the last weekend and every telephone conversation since then, minutely dissecting each nuance to glean if he may have unwittingly offended her. He was aware that the fairer sex, Sara being the fairest of them all, could be very sensitive but he was fairly sure that nothing he had done could have upset her enough to stop her calling. Yet she hadn't called and he couldn't get hold of her. Could she have been involved in an accident? Been mugged? Raped?? He would surely have heard by now. God, it was a nightmare; his poor baby! The only thing for it was to drive to Exeter; he could do it in, a very illegal, three hours if he put his foot down.

34

He was just about to put this plan into action when his mobile rang. He answered it before the first ring had finished.

"Sara?"

"Hi Hugo, sorry no, it's Maggie."

"Oh my God! What's happened?" Hugo managed to blurt out, anxiety overwhelming him.

"Please don't worry, Sara has just got some sort of flu bug" she replied, trying to relax him. "I went into her room to borrow her hair dryer this morning and she was a bit hot and woozy."

"Oh my God!" he repeated "Have you called the doctor? Does she need to be admitted into hospital? I'll come over immediately. I was gathering my things when you called."

"Yes I called the doctor and he came very quickly actually" Maggie said reassuringly,

"He said there's a lot of flu about and that she'll be right as rain in a few days. He told us to make sure she drinks enough water and keep her cool." She sensibly chose not to tell him that her temperature was over thirty-nine degrees.

"Please don't bother coming over. She's not very with it any way and there's no point you catching it too. She'll need you healthy when she's convalescing. Lucy and 1 are here this weekend so we can look after her. And anyway, she hasn't showered or washed her hair today and would never forgive us if we let you see her like this!"

He felt torn. He wanted to be with her for selfish reasons because he missed her so much and because he wanted to take care of her but could see the sense of staying well for when she needed him.

"Well, if you're sure" he said reluctantly, "please will you call me with updates and tell her I love her and am thinking of her?"

"Of course, please try not to worry, Hugo, Lucy and I are very capable, you know."

"I know and thank you so much for phoning, I was getting myself into a real state!"

That had been clear from their conversation and the little Maggie knew of him. Where Sara was concerned, he was very over the top. It was really sweet but would have driven her pots!

"I knew you would be, take care"

"And you, thanks again."

35

His poor baby! He was, of course, still very worried about her but also exceedingly relieved at the same time that his greater fears had been unsubstantiated. He really most stop getting himself in such a tizzy, that couple of hours had been hell, like part of him were missing; the pain of missing her had felt almost physical. And now he would have to wait another whole seven days till he could see her. What was he going to do with himself?

....

Rupert was having a wonderful weekend; he wished it could always be like this. He couldn't remember being quite so elated. There was no ridiculous feathery thing flapping about and he had Hugo all to himself; this was as blissful as it got. Hugo had got up late as expected giving Rupert plenty of time to reorganise the office filing cabinets and read the Financial Times from cover to cover. The pink paper was delivered daily and whilst rarely if ever touched by Hugo, was always at least scanned by his employee.

As soon as Rupert had heard movement from upstairs he'd finished preparing a full English breakfast, two rounds of buttered thick granary toast and a large decaffeinated cafe mocha as a treat for the master. It worked. Hugo who had appeared looking very down in the mouth visibly brightened as soon as he saw his feast.

"What a banquet! Thank you Rupert." he asked appreciatively "I didn't know how talented you are! You're a star, this is wonderful."

"Just thought you might be missing Sara and need cheering up, old bean" Rupert was excellent at feigning empathy when it served his purpose or pleased someone he liked to be pleasant to. He'd learned that it seemed to offend people when he was simply honest and that fitting into any sort of society or social grouping demanded a little play acting. Well so be it, if that smoothed things along.

"Then thank you, it's very kind of you. It's rather a rum weekend without poor Sara but seeing as you're about, there's something I've been meaning to talk to you about." Rupert's heart sank; what could this be? Was it something to do with Sara? He could only keep this act up for so long.

36

"It's about the housekeeper, gardener and what-have-you. I don't want to burden you but you're better with them than I am and I wondered if you'd be prepared to take their management off me? For further remuneration of course."

Rupert couldn't believe his ears, this was simply amazing news! No Sara and now jurisdiction over the staff. What a marvellous weekend!

"I'd be happy to Sir, and no extra remuneration is necessary."

"Well then that's settled...and less of the 'sir' please" Hugo smiled indulgently. This man was a miracle and for that he could put up with a few sir-type idiosyncrasies.

. . . .

The house was silent; no music and no chatter meant Sara's housemates were out. She stood up groggily, steadying herself on the bedstead. The room swayed a little but not so much as it had been doing and she was more than fed up with being in bed and feeling grimy. She'd greedily eaten the sandwich the sweet girls had left for her and she hadn't even worked out the calories; she'd reckoned her body deserved it after several days fasting. She looked down at her tummy; it was concave. Excellent, this being ill thing wasn't so bad after all, she smiled weakly. Maggie and Lucy had also plugged her phone into the charger by her bed. What darlings they were, they'd really looked after her. She never actually socialised with them but they had shared convivially enough when they'd all moved out of the university halls and the two friends had needed someone to share living costs with; she had synchronistically overheard them discussing it and they had decided to move in to the three bedroomed terrace that they'd continued to rent this year.

She looked in the dressing table mirror. Big mistake! Thank goodness Hugo hadn't been there to see her; Maggie had told her he'd wanted to come but she'd been able to stop him, thank God. She missed him more than anything but this really was not a good look and he'd had to be spared! She dragged herself to the shower and carefully, tentatively washed her frail, overly sensitive body and lank hair. She still ached but the sting of the water on her skin and the

37

soreness of her scalp were more bearable than feeling so unwashed for another second.

After patting herself dry with her fluffiest towel she dressed herself in comfortable, baggy clothes that were even baggier on her empty body and tried softly drawing a brush through her hair, compromising with less efficient but less uncomfortable fingers. Worn out, she lay on the bed and day dreamed about Hugo's party. She could hardly wait to be back in London; she loved her life there. The only thing that marred her time there was the omnipresent and freakily weird Rupert who had an uncanny way of making out that he was giving them their space whist always seeming to be lurking about behind the scenes somehow. It was totally beyond her why Hugo liked and relied upon him so much. He truly creeped her out and she ardently hoped to be able to persuade Hugo to make him move out before she moved in. She felt reasonably confident he would comply with her wishes, considering how much he loved her but she'd much prefer him to be happy about it. Surely that would be ok? After all, most personal assistants didn't live in and Hugo could easily afford to pay him more to make up for the accommodation loss. Maybe she would broach the subject this weekend when Hugo was extra pleased to see her; Rupert was just too odd for her to be comfortable sharing the house with.

. . . .

Hugo was madly excited. Sara was on her way over for the first time in two whole weeks and he was going to show her off at their party tomorrow. He'd missed her more than he could say, it was well over a year since they had gone so long without each other and it had been horrid. He had even cut last year's skiing trip down from his usual fourteen to six days and timed it carefully so as not to be away from her for too long. In future he would take her with him of course; he loved the idea of teaching her how to ski and snowboard, he knew she would be brilliant at both. He smiled happily at the amazing future they would have, there were so, so many wonderful things ahead of them! He had to make sure that they were never separated again like this again and whilst he felt eternally grateful to

Maggie and Lucy for looking after his sweetheart, he knew for certain that he couldn't allow her to be away from him and vulnerable ever again.

With a deep breath he decided for definite that he would ask her father for Sara's hand in marriage at Christmas. Gosh, now he'd made that resolution he was even more nervous about meeting her parents and fervently hoped that he would be considered good enough for their pride and joy, their precious little girl. It sounded a bit formal and old fashioned to ask for David's permission but felt that things had to be done correctly; Rupert would be proud of him! Their wedding, the exchanging of vows and the start of their married life together was going to be a very reverent and magical occasion and every detail, starting with this one, had to be planned with great care. He knew it would be impractical to hurry the arrangements for the big day or to deprive his bride of her anticipation. The whole wedding planning thing was pretty much a mystery to him but he knew that both his future mother-in-law and his own mother would need time to do whatever was necessary to create the perfect day for their nuptials; and a perfect it was certainly going to be. Both he and Sara were only children so their co-joining in holy matrimony would be very special to both sets of parents and, he hoped, a new lease of life for hers.

He had never held with the unfair tradition that a bride's parents paid for everything and in any case his folks were in a better position financially to fund it. He hoped that this would take any pressure off the Bramptons and not make them feel uncomfortable at all; he would need to handle the subject delicately. However long the organisation had to take and therefore the length of their engagement had to be, he knew now that he had to initiate it much sooner rather than later. If this fortnight had taught him anything, it was that he needed to put himself in the position of her permanent protector as soon as humanly possible. Her father permitting and he hoped that would be just a formality, he could propose on New Year's Day so he must start looking for a ring! Excitedly, he daydreamed about a two coloured gold one with a large solitaire diamond; he wanted her ring to sparkle as much as he knew his bride would. He determined to start looking on Monday when Sara would be back in Exeter. It was a huge secret to keep but he wanted it to be a surprise. He would probably have to visit a lot of jewellers to get exactly what he had in mind but he wasn't prepared to compromise. She could move in as soon as she had completed her final exams in June; as a betrothed couple he hoped it would be considered completely seemly, even by her parents, for her then to reside with him full time. There was a spare suite where she kept a lot of her clothes already and he believed that would satisfy appearances until after the wedding. For two pins, he'd have her move in with him immediately; she didn't need her degree as he would see to it that she'd never have to lift a finger again in her life but his sensible self knew how many sacrifices her family had made for her education and that she must complete it.

. . . .

Sara had hardly noticed the journey; she knew the route and the routine so well that it appeared she could go through it with hardly a conscious thought. The train had been waiting at the platform early when she'd arrived and the taxi had been there for her at Paddington with its usual efficiency. She supposed that at this time of year there must have been a plethora of Christmas lights, decorations and trees on the way which she would normally have been mesmerised by but it seemed that she had travelled all the way from Paddington station to South Kensington in a blur of post illness haze and her own thoughts because she had noticed none. She had slept for the entire train journey having set the alarm on her phone for ten minutes before arrival; she had heard of too many horror stories from friends about sleeping through their stops and arriving in Edinburgh and such like. Even though London Paddington was the final destination she thought it easily possible one might not be detected and just stay on and travel all the way back to Exeter and beyond it to Plymouth! Whilst she slept she'd left her ticket on the table where the conductor could see it so as not to be disturbed. She could well imagine it might have been stolen elsewhere on the train but she'd thankfully been correct in her assumption that wouldn't happen in first class.

Rupert looked at his watch, exhaled deeply and breathed in the last of the silence he knew couldn't for much longer. It had been so pleasant for the past twelve days but he aware that it would be as though she hadn't been away as soon as she arrived. He could tell that he was already tense about her imminent arrival because he was making and repeating..and repeating..and repeating to-do lists in his mind. This habit could usually be alleviated by writing down the activities he needed to perform but he'd tried that and his brain was still insisting on uncomfortably obsessing about every single task to be completed over and over.

"Sara's here!" called Hugo elatedly, in that silly voice he reserved for such occasions "Come and say hi."

Rupert rolled his eyes, clenched his fists, resignedly walked out into the reception hall, formed what he hoped was a suitable smile and lightly air kissed each of the skinny dwarf's cheeks. He carefully and painfully held his mask until he had turned away and was walking back to his apartment thirty long seconds later. He locked and bolted his door behind him and stood leaning his back against it whilst trying to slow his breathing and settle the helter-skelter of his mind. As soon as he felt steady he took a seat in his armchair and listened to Bach's soothing 'Goldberg Variations' by which time he was ready for his beloved 'Clarinet Concerto', one of Mozart's final works. He could feel the stress flowing away and fairly soon he was ready to have a bath, necessarily clean his bathroom and then get an early night.

....

Sara raised her eyebrows at Rupert's extremely stilted greeting and mouthed to Hugo

"He's so weird!"

She bit her lip to avoid swearing out loud once the freaky little misfit had minced back to his rooms. She tried to be as ladylike as possible in front of Hugo who shrugged apologetically and gave her a 'he's not that bad when you get to know him' look. She was pretty sure that she'd always think he was that bad however well she got to know him. He led her to the sitting room where to all intents and purposes they were alone and they cuddled up on the sofa, enjoying being together after so long. Sara nestled into Hugo's chest and sighed contentedly. She wished she could stay snuggling like this forever; there wasn't any other place in the world she would rather be. She was very much looking forward to the party but was worn out now and extremely relieved they had this evening to just relax together. The flu bug had really knocked it out of her but she forgave it as it had lost her half a stone.

....

Hugo loved nothing better than holding Sara close and feeling protective of her. It was at times like these he felt most at one with her with none of the insecurities he often felt, none of the niggling doubts about her being too good for him, about her leaving him for someone better; he couldn't bear to even think of life without her. He knew that women didn't think or feel in quite the way most men and certainly he could understand and it worried him that he could inadvertently do something that might upset her. But now, like this, he could simply relax and nuzzle into her lovely sweet coconut and vanilla fragranced hair and be the happiest man alive. He kissed her head and asked caringly,

"How's my sweetheart now? Are you sure you're really up to the party? We can still cancel and watch a film tomorrow if you prefer. You really shouldn't push yourself when you've been so poorly"

"Are you crazy baby?" she grinned, "It's very sweet of you to say you'd sacrifice the party you've been looking forward to so much but I'm feeling almost completely back to normal and am dying to wear my new dress. Did I tell you I bought some shoes to go with it?"

"Only a hundred times!" He laughed and tickled her. Sara at once forgot how weak she had been feeling, squirmed out of his grip, knelt on his arms and tickled him back. The two of them horsed around like children, play fighting and squealing until they tumbled off the settee with a loud thud and dissolved into hysterical giggles.

....

Across the hall, in his own quarters, Rupert heard the muffled bang and laughter. His body stiffened and he clamped his teeth together, this was utterly intolerable. Had she not an ounce of self respect or dignity? He was seething. The way she worked her cruel and attention-grabbing enchantment on the poor naive Hugo was painful to watch. She had woven a seemingly all-encompassing web of malevolence around him and he was too sweet and kind to realise. How he loathed and despised her!

. . . .

"Are you ready darling?" Hugo called from the hall, "They'll be here any minute."
When no reply came he strode to the bottom of the stairwell so as to make himself better heard. He opened his mouth but before he could repeat his question she appeared, vision-like, at the top of the stairs. He gasped with his mouth still open as he and time stood still. She seemed to float toward him; her graceful frame even tinier than usual glided effortlessly down the grand staircase whilst her fine hair and the sheer silvery fabric of her dress gently billowed out behind her. She looked like an angel, a goddess. He suddenly realised he must be looking extremely gormless and shut his mouth, pulling himself abruptly back from what had seemed like a trance. He shook himself and remembering his manners and that he hadn't actually spoken yet managed
"You look....you look more beautiful than I have ever seen you." And then "You truly will be the belle of the ball!"
She loved being the centre of his attention, being able to gain that reaction. She liked being his princess but the truth was that she felt just the same about him. She allowed her eyes to slide over him; he looked incredible in his tux. A little thrill of pleasure ran through her as she thought how good he would look out of it later too. She rapidly took control of herself before he was able to guess her thoughts, gave him what she hoped was a sweet and enigmatic ghost of a smile and slid her tiny hand into his. He planted the gentlest of kisses on the gossamer crown of her beautiful head and his heart could have burst with pride. She pushed her little nose into his warm neck and for a moment they were the only two people that existed.

43

Their romantic quiet was abruptly and unceremoniously shattered by a sudden flurry of activity as their guests started appearing. Hugo and Sara greeted their visitors cordially and saw to it that the staff relieved them of their coats and outerwear. Blasts of cold air poured into the hallway with each influx but all the fires were roaring and soon everyone had arrived and the house was warm and full of gentlemen in black tie and ladies in evening wear. Everywhere Sara looked, there were pearls and feathers, silk and velvet, satin and diamante. She loved it! She hadn't met everyone before but she remembered the names of those she had and learned the new ones quickly.

She spent the beginning of the evening introducing people with similar interests and generally being the perfect hostess. Hugo was in awe of the way she so adeptly played the room and how she used her natural socialising and recollection skills so faultlessly. Between introductions she gravitated back to him who was every bit the genial host and in his element catching up with all of his friends. She slid through the throng around him each time and melted into the space beside him. His arms drew her in tightly and the air fizzed between them almost tangibly. She basked in the look of pride and love he exhibited, knowing he was enjoying as much as she, the kindly and indulgent looks from their friends.

. . . .

Rupert, efficient as ever had made a stunning champagne tower from which he gave each new guest a crystal glass from the very top that he kept replenishing to keep the spectacle complete. Everyone around him looked boringly similar in their evening uniforms, the men were all waddling around like long legged penguins and the women could hardly move at all in their stupidly high heels and voluminous or restrictive dresses. They all greedily quaffed the very expensive drink he'd procured on Hugo's behalf like it was cheap squash; surely Hugo could find less frivolous and ungrateful friends? He himself would never loosen his grip on the reins of his self respect and drink alcohol like these pathetic people, he had seen it be

44

a contributing factor in the destruction of his own family and passionately distrusted it. Despite his disapproval he managed to smile convivially at each guest he served. His smirk became actual as he imagined himself as a type of upper class pusher of destitution and suffering as he doled out ruin in the guise of a glass of fizzy liquid. It rather amused him to envision these ridiculous toffs in the gutter with nothing left and needing the staff they could no longer afford to help them.

....

Whatever Hugo may have lacked in the skills of those intelligent and able people he spent his days with he made up for with a relaxed, laid-back manner which put everyone with whom he came into contact at ease. He circulated through the rooms chatting and laughing casually with his dear friends; family accepted, all his favourite people were right here and blissfully, they all looked happy. What more could he ever possibly want? He chuckled as he watched some of his old rowing chums negotiating with their skewers, strawberries and chocolate fountains and in the main part making a terribly good job of staying clean! He felt humbled that so many people had all made an effort to come from their various parts of the country. After spending fifteen minutes catching up the rowers he sauntered over to Jonathan who was guiltily choosing candy sticks from the cart and greeted him warmly with a hand on his back.

"I give you my full permission to let you hair down and enjoy, you can restart your diet tomorrow. How are you my friend?"

"Fabulous thank you. Superb party old chum, let me introduce you to Jane. I hope you don't mind my bringing her along? She knows a few people here and the networking will be good for her."

"I don't mind in the slightest, the more the merrier. Very pleased to meet you, Jane, I've heard a *lot* about you." He air kissed the nice looking but restrained woman who reciprocated hesitantly but smiled warmly. She wore a full length simple but beautifully cut jet black dress with a high neck and long sleeves with flat velvet pumps and no jewellery. Her sleek, dark hair was scraped back into a bun, showing off high, pale cheek bones. He turned aside to Jonathan and whispered

45

"The networking will be good for her?!" he teased. "You didn't need my party to meet your perfect woman. You seem to have done that all by yourself!"

The usually unflappable financial advisor reddened and practically spluttered his denials.

"Don't be ridiculous! I'm her client and that would be...be..unethical" he finished.

Hugo patted him on the back, laughing and genuinely wished him all the luck in the world.

. . . .

The daft children seemed to be playing fairly nicely, nothing had been broken and no one was embarrassingly drunk yet so Rupert made his escape and inserted his earplugs. He felt sullied by such prolonged time in their presence and badly needed to recharge his batteries.

Without him, the party continued on cheerfully and without mishap into the early hours until the last of the guests had asked for their furs and overcoats and bungled themselves into taxis amidst farewells and thank you-s.

. . . .

At a quarter to four Sara and Hugo fell into bed. Sara had all but recovered though was now in much need of sleep; so much for her thoughts of earlier! It had been beyond doubt a truly lovely evening and everyone had seemed to enjoy it as much as they had. One or two had been a little worse for wear by the end but it had been a far more civilised affair than the university parties she was used to.

"I hope you know how much I love you" Hugo mumbled as she curled up sleepily against him.

"Maybe almost as much as I love you." She snuggled in a little closer and if he said anything further, she didn't hear it.....

Chapter Seven

It was seven o'clock on Monday evening so therefore it was run time. Hugo had only ever once missed their 'run date' with the excellent excuse of being on the slopes in Switzerland. He came downstairs wearing running tights, a long sleeved top and a bright lime jacket; it definitely was not shorts and vest weather. He laced up his new lime and purple trainers and pulled on his matching jacket. As long as one was properly clothed and shod the cold wasn't too uncomfortable once you got going but it was a bit grim at first. His father would have told him it was character building and good for his soul; Hugo simply reminded himself that the run justified the large lunch he had enjoyed with his running partner earlier in the day. He wasn't prepared to let himself go and made sure he kept himself in good enough shape for his sweetheart. Thinking of Sara reminded him of the rings he'd seen today. He hadn't found what he'd wanted and if he didn't soon, he would have one made. He'd really missed her today after the wonderful weekend. As well as missing Sara and feeling inadequate because he didn't cope well without her, he'd managed to embarrass himself by leaving cute Labrador puppy pictures on his laptop again and no doubt Rupert had seen them when he'd gone out for lunch. Oh well, the personal assistant would just have to get used to it, he thought with rare rebellion, this was his house and he would fill it with actual puppies when Sara moved in.

He heard Jonathan's familiar rap at the door, bound over and pulled it open with enthusiasm.

"Blimey, you're keen," guffawed Jonathan, taken aback by the speed of the door opening.

"You'll be telling me you're wearing your heart rate monitor next!"

"Hardly! It feels like wearing a bra, er not that I know what wearing a bra feels like!"

"Well I'm glad we've got that straight!" laughed the keener man who had already jogged from where he got off the train he'd taken from his home in Kensal Rise. He would do the same on the way home, unless he felt too tired and jumped on the bus round the corner at Onslow Gardens. Either way, it was a good extra thirty minutes in each direction.

Hugo no longer threw himself religiously into sport. At university, he had taken his fitness very seriously, been into all the recommended supplements and gadgets, attended the gym most days and was captain of his rowing club. He'd loved it but his rowing buddies had dispersed and he now had different priorities. Other than the twice weekly runs and the sit ups and press ups he did most days, he now did comparatively little. He had occasionally wondered if he should convert part of the cellar into a weights room but he knew that would mean having to work on his claustrophobia first. To date he had never really felt sufficiently motivated to face his fear but he was thinking more and more about restarting a regular weight training routine and it would be so much more convenient to exercise at home. His naturally good physique was easy to maintain at his age but it couldn't be sustained forever and he knew Sara liked his body in shape. Before he could have hypnotherapy to cure his dread of enclosed spaces though, he would have to have hypnotherapy to cure his fear of hypnotherapy! Thinking of hypnotherapy caused him to turn to his friend mischievously,

"So.... what's going on with you and the marvel Jane?"

After a slightly longer pause than necessary, Jonathan ventured a simple

"Nothing."

"You really think I'm going to let you off with that? Come on, spill the beans"

"Well" Jonathan started slowly, "between you and me, I've got myself rather smitten but that's as far as it goes. Jane is much too professional to see a client romantically and in any case she's in a very different league to me."

"Nonsense, you're an excellent catch! Give her time, I'm sure she'll succumb to your charms soon enough and I don't see why it would be unethical, you're not undergoing treatment with her anymore."

"Maybe....." he sounded dubious. "We're not all lucky like you. Sara's obviously as besotted with you as you are with her, the two of you looked really loved up on Saturday. I noticed you couldn't keep your eyes off each other even when you were both mingling at opposite ends of the room."

Hugo had been bursting to talk about his decision but hadn't wanted to be impolite by jumping in too soon with his own stuff. He now felt able to say,

"I want to tell you something important," he paused dramatically before delivering his impressive news, "I'm going to talk to Sara's father when we visit at Christmas because I intend to propose to her on New Year's Day and move her in with me as soon as she finishes her degree whilst we prepare for the big day." Hearing himself say the words out loud gave them a gravity and importance that made him feel very proud indeed. Jonathan almost slowed his pace to an unprecedented standstill. "I'm so very, very pleased for you, you're the perfect couple! It's such excellent news; we need to think about celebrating."

"We will," Hugo squeaked excitedly "but let's just get her 'yes' first, shall we?"

They picked up speed and chatted gleefully for a while until Hugo realised his right big toe was really quite painful and that his new trainers were rubbing a lot. Fortunately they were very nearly back at the Square and Hugo's house. Jonathan waved as he jogged off into the distance. Hugo hobbled upstairs, showered and administered some Germolene and a sticking plaster to his blistered toe. He donned his favourite cosy leisure suit and settled down for a quiet and relaxing evening of doing absolutely nothing.

....

What the hell was that dreadful racket? Hugo had nearly leapt out of his skin! An almost inhuman wailing which seemed to permeate the entire building had broken out somewhere below him and was steadily crescendoing. Adrenalin pumped through his veins as he bounded down the stairs alarmed for his household's safety, not knowing what to expect but fearing the worst and being prepared to

49

take on whatever faced him. He arrived in the hall breathless to find that Rupert was already there, looking coolly and disdainfully at the perpetrator; the housekeeper.

"What on earth is going on??" Hugo demanded curtly, his heart still pounding.

"I'm so sorry you were disturbed Hugo, please allow me to take care of this." Rupert managed to sound both condescending and disingenuous despite the politeness of his words. When Hugo didn't make any move to retreat, the newly appointed manager of the staff continued,

"Please go and continue your evening. I'm afraid I found this disobedient and supercilious specimen smoking a cigarette in the pantry and obviously I had to give her marching orders. I explained that her behaviour was classed as gross misconduct and that she must leave the premises immediately but, as you can hear, she is not taking it graciously though - why I would have expected any sense of decorum from these people I do not know."

Mrs Cappott's crying was getting louder, if that were possible, causing Hugo to feel even more greatly out of his depth. He shifted uncomfortably from one foot to the other as the woman ranted incoherently between sobs. Rupert, in contrast, was a tranquil pool of calmness.

"Really, sir, get some rest," he now spoke reassuringly "this will be sorted out in two shakes of a lamb's tail."

Hugo wasn't reassured; the air crackled with tension. He didn't like confrontation; it was excruciating and worried him immensely. He had always done all he could to avoid it; in fact, this was actually the first time he'd witnessed such dysfunctional an interaction and he was finding it deeply unpleasant. Nothing like this had ever taken place in his presence before and he thought such occurrences were purely fictional and restricted to the genre of soap operas and the like. Putting his own discomfort to one side for a moment, the altruistic part of him hated to see anyone so upset, let alone out of a job just before Christmas especially when he himself had employed them and had known them for quite some considerable time. He had always found the woman to be extremely agreeable whenever he had come into contact with her and yet it was true that he strictly and fervently disallowed cigarettes in the house. So against the practice was he, that he had checked that she was a non smoker when he'd first interviewed her; this must be a new habit. It was also the case, he reasoned, that he had passed this kind of responsibility onto Rupert, partly, he supposed because of the possibility of this sort of situation. He was in such a dreadful quandary but maybe he should probably just allow Rupert to get on with his job. The whole state of affairs felt to him to be very wrong but the man had always been a good decision maker and never let him down before after all.

The huge relief that Hugo had felt whilst slowly backing away and escaping into the peace and safety of his bedroom, was tainted slightly by a faint but gnawing primeval feeling that he had somehow lost his alpha male status. He told himself that he was being silly of course, that Rupert was his employee and simply providing a service that the richer man needed and was fortunately able to afford. The man was obviously merely following instructions and efficiently carrying out his tasks.....and yet the niggling thoughts of changing dynamics and loss of power continued to linger for the rest of the evening, distracting from his relaxation even more than the throbbing in his toe.

. . . .

At eleven o'clock in the morning of the day following the previous evening's victory over the household, Rupert was quietly celebrating alone with the cappuccino he had treated himself to whilst the master drank his earl grey. He thought he might even push the boat out further and have a digestive. He approved and defended this almost unprecedented frivolity as he held that his successful assertion of authority as staff manager deserved commemorating; it was now understood that he was a force to be recognised. Never having been one to push himself forward, always having preferred to obtain his self respect through service, he had to admit now to the thrill of excitement that came with the assertion of power and he puffed out his chest. His phone ringing interrupted his reverie.

Looking at the screen, he recognised the number as a gentleman from the other side of the Square who was retiring to the Maldives.

He hoped that this was the good news he'd wished for since taking the initiative to call him first thing this morning. After a short but successful negotiation he took four measured strides to the biscuit tin and obtained himself two digestives...and a rich tea. Only sixteen hours after having expelled the arrogant and foolish housekeeper he had replaced her with a self effacing little creature who shared none of her predecessor's grandiose delusions of untouchability. She brought with her excellent credentials and her employer, due to his imminent emigration, had been prepared to release her almost immediately. She would live out and come in to cook every evening. He could easily cater for the rest; breakfast was rarely more than cereals or a piece of toast and lunch was either sandwiches, soup or eaten out. Rupert intended to clearly lay down his rules of employment to his first member of staff when she came over for an interview later that day and he planned to ask her to make dinner tomorrow evening by way of a trial. From a very brief meeting he'd had with her, he had gleaned that unlike the woman he'd had to cleanse the house of, this gentle lady, diminutive in demeanour as well as stature would be satisfactorily compliant. Now they just needed a cleaner but hiring one could easily wait till the New Year. It was only two weeks till Christmas when Hugo would be away for a good few days and Rupert was more than capable of keeping the place ship shape for the time being.

. . . .

Rupert sat back in his chair, surveyed his apartment and let out a sigh. It was beautifully peaceful and almost impossible to believe they were so relatively close to the hub of the city. He looked at his watch and exhaled again. It was irksome that the scrawny one was due any second now. Still, he wasn't going to allow the emaciated Sara to ruin his good mood and in any case he was happy in his own company and intended to spend the next two days cataloguing his compact discs. He had rather an impressive operatic and classical collection and looked forward to the catharsis of the task. Almost as soon as he had enjoyed that positive thought the cacophony of the front door slamming resounded noisily through the house and each of his nerve cells interrupting his tranquillity and causing him to jolt bolt upright. He shuddered and wondered how such a scraggy bird of a woman could cause so much disruption and commotion. He sat back again, shut out best he could the hullabaloo and absorbed himself in his own deliberations.

During his introspective moments, Rupert liked to imagine a life where the stick insect stray didn't exist, where he could live out his peaceful and contented existence without the continual and tiresome interruption of her visits. His life here with Hugo would be perfect if the weekends were as Sara free as the other days of the week. He liked their Monday to Friday routine and had no doubt that the master could easily get over his strange addiction to her. He had no clue at all why the master thought he enjoyed her presence, he assumed that there was sexual gratification and he shuddered at the very idea of being so close to another person. He understood that most men were weak and unable to satisfy their requirements alone but he saw the act as disgusting and he couldn't see that it could possibly be worth putting up with a woman's inane and complete foolishness. It was unseemly and undignified and he hated that he had been conceived in that way. A world of clones or the use of artificial insemination would be much cleaner and more proper; the whole method of coupling and procreation was repellent.

His noticed that he was clenching his jaw and fists. Females who allowed men to do this to them were nothing other than dirty sluts and how could one respect that? Respect any woman therefore? He must calm down; as it often happened, his happy musings had been completely and nauseatingly hijacked by these darker thoughts and he could feel the familiar and escalating feelings of confusion, of disgust and of fear. He loathed these feelings, was shocked by their growing intensity and regularity, felt furious with himself for not controlling them. Control was ones only true defence against the nameless powers that threatened to unsettle ones equilibrium...

He took a very deep breath to slow his heart rate, shook himself physically and mentally, picked up a Puccini CD and carefully adhered a small white sticker to its right hand upper corner. Once numbered, its title and notation were entered into the moleskin notebook he had bought expressly for this purpose. Losing himself in this type of ordered activity afforded him the calm he craved and he managed to spend a contented while slaying the demons which had reeked chaos in both his CD collection and his mind. For a short time he felt almost at peace until the feeling of absorbing himself therapeutically in ordering and categorising wrenched him disturbingly back to his childhood when he could remember he had hummed whilst compulsively tidying his Lego collection with the aim of blanking out his mother's rants and sobs. To his horror he realised that at twenty-four he was humming now.

That vicious little sprite had done this to him, unsettled him like this, it was because of she that he was dredging up the past. He *must* control it. Control was everything. Control was everything. Control was everything. From the other side of his door he could hear the two inconsiderate and wicked devils absurdly cackling and running around. He hummed louder and louder.

. . . .

Rupert found overt displays of emotion, indeed any displays of emotion distasteful. He distrusted so called love and believed people were pitiable for allowing themselves to become embroiled with another. He believed that all people were flawed in some way and that joining and magnifying those dysfunctions could only lead to the emergence of pain, loneliness and destruction. His mother and father had spent twenty years together and would no doubt have stayed together for several decades longer had the 'death do us part' element of their marriage ceremony not materialised prematurely. They had stayed together despite all the many flaws his mother had brought to the partnership and no doubt several of his father's. What had been the point? He knew not of their relationship before his arrival but presumably something constructive must have existed between them at one time but, if it had, he certainly never saw any evidence of it.

His mother had no doubt stayed in the unhappy union because she had no other option, only being able to take on sporadic casual jobs which she always had to leave. Maybe his father had held a misplaced sense of duty or perhaps apathy had simply held him in its unhealthy grip. More likely, the continual fire fighting against the ogre of his mother's mental impairments had overshadowed the mere spectre of a poor marriage. Rupert had watched the lack of fulfilment and joy gnaw away at them. Had he ever seen even a spark of contentment between them, he might have been more able to understand a purpose of relationships or why his father had reacted in the way he had in the end. As it was, he'd had no other option than to see his father's final feeble action for what it obviously was; a thoughtless, weak and cruel act.

Chapter Eight

Sara was having a really lovely week which was very unusual when she wasn't with Hugo. Two of the girls from her course, Charlotte and Emily had always seemed more smiley, less judgemental and certainly much more fashionable than the rest but Sara had always made it her policy not to interact with any of the other students. It was her way of protecting herself from the bitchiness and back biting she had experienced from the girls at school. Sixty percent of her science course was predictably male but although they were obviously more attentive to her than the girls, she wasn't inclined to trust the intentions of their shallow and immature friendliness either. It had always been easier and safer to keep herself to herself, but on Tuesday she had found herself uncharacteristically drawn to comment on a discussion that Charlotte and Emily had been sharing about shoes.

This had lead onto a rather long three way conversation about the relative merits of the most convenient handbags to use on campus. It seemed that the three of them shared a preoccupation with the very problematic task of discovering a bag which was both practical and fashionable and they had managed to happily chat about the pros and cons of various designers and other shared interests for more than a couple of hours. For Sara, it had been remarkable and blissful to simply talk with girls so comfortably, allowing their conversation to drift and meander with ease. By the lunch time they had had the beginnings of a good relationship. By the time they had shared a salad and each drunk a fruit tea in a cafe surrounded by carol singers and twinkly lights, they were firm friends. She hadn't ever had female or indeed any friends before and this new novelty was going to make her final term so much more fun. She felt blessed and complete, which led her thoughts to Hugo. Though she was nervous, she was incredibly excited about going with her lovely boyfriend to visit his family residence for Christmas. She could hardly wait to meet all his relatives and be shown around the house Hugo had grown up in. She was also thrilled about introducing him to her parents and generally spending the longest time she had ever spent with him. It would feel like they were a proper couple. She was always childishly energized about the yuletide period but this year was going to be extra, extra special and then rather than dread her enforced but inevitable separation from Hugo and the impending boredom of studying, she would have the growing of her new friendship to look forward to.

Sara happily waved au revoir to Emily and Charlotte as they started walking to the flat they shared just on the edge of campus and she got into a taxi to her house which was quite a bit further away but walkable by most students. They were all going to shower and change before meeting again to go out for a calorie friendly light meal at Yo! Sushi and then on to a bar. They had agreed that they could each have one cocktail, as long as it didn't contain cream, to celebrate and cement their new friendship. They had also already arranged to meet in the sports centre early the next morning in order to burn off as many of the calories as they could.

Once in the cab, Sara rooted through the oversized DKNY bag which contained all her essentials, eventually retrieving her iPhone by feel from under everything else inside the dark interior. The inconvenience of this type of time consuming rummaging had formed one of their discussions earlier that day. Oh no! She had had several missed calls from Hugo and six texts saying how worried he was and asking and then begging her to please, please call and reassure him that she was ok and hadn't succumbed to another dangerous ailment or worse.

Her poor boyfriend really did care and worry about her, bless him and she felt extremely guilty, not only that she had not called him earlier but that her phone had been on silent whilst she had been busy enjoying herself. She called him immediately and apologised profusely for not getting in touch earlier and for worrying him, told him how very much she missed and loved him and enthused over her new friendship with the girls.

Hugo was immensely relieved she was ok and he was more than happy to listen to her excited stories. Even if he could have got a word in edgeways he didn't yet feel ready to talk about the housekeeper incident as he still wasn't entirely sure how he himself felt about it. He was even happier than usual to just listen to the pretty, sing-song cadence of her voice and hear the animated account of her day. He was genuinely glad that she had finally found friends at university and had truly never liked to think of her alone in Exeter, save for Maggie and Lucy but though he tried he couldn't quite push away the slight concern that he may be becoming a tad superfluous. It was rather unsettling that nobody actually seemed to need him anymore.

Hugo had been so quiet on the phone. Sara knew he was upset and that she was utterly responsible, she really should have spoken to him earlier in the day and not been so wrapped up in her own pursuits. After all, she knew how insecure he could get even though she'd never understood it when he was so gorgeous. It had been really mean and selfish of her to ignore him and she felt terrible. She never wanted him to feel hurt and certainly never wanted to be the cause of his pain. She would have to think of a way to make it up to him, to make him feel loved and valued again and she must remember to be more sensitive in future. She couldn't say she wasn't absolutely thrilled about having proper friends at last but it was a little like being excited about parties and dresses; it couldn't possibly be compared to the depth of love she felt for the soul mate she had found in Hugo and she wouldn't dream of swapping him for the entire world.

. . . .

It had been four days since Sara had made friends with Charlotte and Emily and they had already been to the gym, the sauna, the library and out shopping as well as preparing and eating dinner together at the girls' flat. As if this hadn't been exciting enough, she was now off to spend the whole of the holidays with Hugo *and* it was only fourteen more sleeps until Christmas day! What a wonderful, wonderful life she had. Her huge Ralf Lauren suit case standing to heel at her side whilst she waited for the cab made her feel that it really was holiday time. Usually an overnight bag was all that was necessary because she kept a set of toiletries and other essentials in London but she'd needed to pack properly for the whole Christmas period. Living in two places had become second nature to her but there was often something she had forgotten to duplicate that was in the house that she wasn't. Fortunately she never minded shopping for replacements.

The car arrived on time as always and the driver, one of her favourites, hoisted her large case into his boot as she settled herself into the back seat. They chatted pleasantly about their respective Christmas plans until the taxi drew into St. David's car park just eight minutes later.

As she entered the station, only twenty minutes before her 16:03 Paddington train was due to depart, she suddenly realised she hadn't brought the gift she'd bought for Hugo and halted abruptly in her tracks causing a rather inconvenient knock on effect in the busy foyer. Apologising to the three people who'd tumbled over her case, she wondered desperately if there was anyone who could meet her here with the present. There wasn't; Maggie and Lucy had unfortunately already left for their parents' houses. She cursed under her breath at her stupidity. Even though Hugo and she had spoken several times since she had thoughtlessly ignored his calls and he had insisted he wasn't upset, she still felt bad so had bought a little teddy holding a pink velvet heart with an 'H' on it. It was a really sweet little bear and she was sad she wasn't now able to give it to him. She had bought him a pair of beautiful cufflinks for Christmas which she knew were stowed safely inside their little box in the internal pocket of her handbag but had wanted to give him a little 'apology and I love you' token tonight.

It was always a bit of a nightmare buying presents for someone who had everything and could afford anything he wanted even though he didn't ever put any pressure on her. The sweetheart had said that he would be more than happy just to have her by his side at

Christmas and consider her smile when she unwrapped the present he'd bought for her a gift enough but he deserved something special. The cufflinks were only gold plated and the diamonds weren't real but they were vintage and looked elegant.

It was now only eighteen minutes to her train and she still had to get across the bridge to platform five. Normally she'd quickly run up the stairs but today with her case she'd have to wait for two lifts and still needed to buy a little snack for the journey not having had anything since the banana at breakfast. She had to be extra careful because it might not be easy to get out of eating later and in any case, she needed to get her weight down as much as possible so as to be able to eat a Christmas lunch without disaster. There were no shops here other than a newsagent and she sighed, accepting she would have to give up on the idea of replacing the teddy. Maddeningly, she wouldn't have time to buy anything at Paddington either because the taxi, which was on contract always met her straight from her train. Growling to herself, she quickly bought a packet of lightly sea salted Propercorn from the cafe and made a mental note to enter the 88kcal onto the list on her phone. She pushed the popcorn into her bag, hurried into the lift, over the bridge that spanned all the lines and down the lift on the other side in time to be seated and looking out of the window of the first class carriage as the guard blew his whistle.

As always, when she got to the taxi rank above platform twelve at twenty-five past six, a car from the reliable firm was already waiting for her. As she trundled her case toward it, the driver kindly came down a little way to meet her with a polite "Good evening Miss, let me help you with that" and took it off her before stowing it quickly and efficiently into his boot. They drove, listening to Radio 1 and occasionally commenting on it, through barely thinning rush hour traffic for nearly an hour to do a journey that would take twenty minutes at a quiet time but, as he pointed out, if you lived in London that was how it was.

As much as she liked the beauty, greenness and space of Exeter and the area surrounding it, especially Dartmoor and some of the quieter beaches, she felt the familiar buzz of the capital city growing within her. She loved the bustle, the cacophony of car horns and music, the imposing buildings, the myriad of colour, diversity of culture and ethnicity and the way, stylistically, so many people made a gesture as well as an effort with their appearance very rarely found in the southwest.

As they approached SW10 the traffic cleared and they found themselves away from the flurry of activity and surrounded by a genteel sophistication which hung in the air with cleansing simplicity. Sara adored it here even more than she did the fun of the city and she could feel her happiness levels rising almost to fever pitch as they swung into Redcliffe Square and Hugo's gorgeous pale stoned townhouse came into view. She swiftly gathered up her bag, alighted from the taxi and bounded up the short flight of steps to the porticoed entrance before the driver had even opened his door to collect her case. She was just about to put her key in the brass lock when the gloss ebony door was flung open and she was being swung round in Hugo's strong arms. What a lovely welcome! Ten minutes later they were cuddled up on the claret coloured velvet chesterfield drinking hot chocolate with floating marshmallows punctuating the narration of their weeks with little kisses and nose nuzzles. Even though they spoke several times each day on the phone, they never seemed to run out of things to share when they got together.

Rupert could hear them periodically laughing and play fighting. It was becoming beyond exasperating. That absurd woman had the poor man wrapped round her little finger and had the infuriating knack of turning the sensible, pleasant man into an idiot! It had been cringe worthy enough to have found ridiculous images of 'cute' animals on the man's laptop but this giggling was just embarrassing. He knew that Hugo would very much prefer him to be on friendly terms with her but whilst he would like to please his employer, even pretending any affiliation was easier said than done. He felt that he had probably allowed his dislike of the woman to cause him to judge his master adversely recently and supposed it would be a kindness to maybe make more of an effort as it was a giving time of year. The very beginnings of a thought were forming in his mind. He slowly and rhythmically nodded to himself; yes it could be a kindness.

Hugo's mobile vibrated. He looked at it, groaned and stood up.

"Sorry sweetheart, I'm going to have to talk to this guy." He grimaced.

I'll go upstairs because I left the paperwork there. It's probably going to be a bit of a long call so make yourself at home and I'll be back for cuddles before you know it." he planted a kiss on the top of her beautiful golden head and slid reluctantly out of her embrace.

"I'm such a lucky girl to have you baby." She mouthed with the sweetest of smiles as he answered his phone.
He blew a silent kiss as backed away toward the door, watching her for as long as he could. She blew him another kiss and mouthed, somewhat guiltily,

"Is the weirdo about?"

"Haven't seen him" he mouthed back, shaking his head, "relax...and be thinking what you'd like to eat tonight and about getting the tree and mistletoe tomorrow!"

Sara felt a little cold with no one to snuggle up to despite the cosy cashmere sweater and pashmina that had been presents from Hugo when he hadn't been able to resist her in the soft, pale cyclamen. The fire in the elegant marble fireplace was beginning to die down and she'd never found herself very skilled at reviving embers but would ask her knight in shining armour to rekindle it as soon as he returned from his phone call. Shivering slightly she pulled the chenille throw from the arm of the sofa and wrapped its cosiness around her tiny shoulders sighing blissfully. The only thing that bit into her peacefulness was the disappointment and frustration that she still felt about forgetting the cute teddy; she could so kick herself. She heard footsteps in the hall and looked up excitedly thinking Hugo was back early but her heart which had leapt, suddenly plummeted when she realised it was only Rupert. What on earth was he doing coming in here? He usually avoided any sort of contact with her like the plague.

He entered the lounge and walked hesitantly toward her, stealing his way up to making what felt to him like an enormous gesture to please Hugo. Never any type of conversationalist, believing any gratuitous or superfluous communication to be facile, boring and unnecessary, the "How are you today? You look a little chilly, can I get you a hot water bottle?" was as hard as some people might have found skydiving.

Sara was stunned by this unprecedented approach; in the eighteen months she'd been visiting here, the two of them had never yet had any kind of normal conversation and she felt that they didn't know each other at all. She felt so far off her guard from the shock of his enquiry and kindness that she simply gabbled to him about having forgotten the stuffed toy, only realising at the station and wishing she had a gift. For an uncomfortable moment silence stood before them. Sara looked down at her hands and bit her lip.

Rupert felt both overwhelmed and intimidated by the sheer number and speed of words that could spill out of her vacuous little mouth and sorely wished that he hadn't started upon this foolhardy debacle. He had learned enough about social etiquette though to know that humming audibly right now would be considered inappropriate so he hummed as loudly as he could inside his head. Her lips appeared to have stopped moving but he felt too paralysed to do anything but look at her wordlessly until the hush became almost tangible. The stillness breaking sentence that flowed from him next shocked them both equally.
"I can help you with a surprise for him" he said and even managed a smile. That smile, to Sara, bridged what she thought had been an impossible and impassable chasm. She felt a warmth; the starting of a bond she had thought unfeasible between them as she sensed the tremendous effort he was making and saw how very much he must want to be friendly to break through what she now realised must be such an appalling shyness.

Rupert tried to keep his thin lips curled into the unfamiliar shape for as long as he could as she seemed to be reacting well to it. He didn't really feel emotion, had never understood it but had learned that if he didn't act the way that people expected, he didn't get what he wanted. The repellent creature was smiling ever more encouragingly; his acting seemed to be producing real results here and his own stretched grin became almost genuine. He allowed himself to forget the altruism he had meant to exhibit for Hugo's sake as he remembered that there could be another kindness he could show him instead.

Chapter Nine

"I ordered more champagne than we needed for the party" Rupert told her "so you could give him one of those, or you could choose a bottle of wine with an appropriate date maybe?" He found it surprisingly easy to pretend to be nice once he had got started. "I'm sure I can even find a bow too with the Christmas things I was looking at yesterday."

He felt as though he were dreaming; was he really going to live out a half formed glimmer of a fantasy? This felt too easy. Was he managing to lull himself into a false sense of security? He hadn't had time to consider all the implications of this thoroughly and couldn't afford to make any mistakes. He'd be much happier if he felt prepared; he'd really have to think quickly on his feet.

"Thank you, this is so helpful of you" she enthused. Way too easy, like taking candy from a baby. If he believed in signs then this was surely telling him he was on the right path at the right time.

"Follow me" he replied "I presume you haven't been in the cellar before? There's a good staircase and extensive lighting but I'm afraid we have to go through the rear porch which is terribly cold at this time of year." He spoke more reassuringly as he noticed a shadow of doubt flicker across her mouse-like features. He smiled again; he was excelling himself!

"Thank you, I'm really grateful to you" she repeated and she was. She almost skipped along after him, delighted to have a gift for Hugo. It wasn't ideal as she knew that Hugo had paid for it but he wouldn't know, she hadn't done it intentionally and it was the thought that counted.

Rupert opened the back porch door and politely held it open for the doll like creature who followed him, shivering at the lowered temperature. With keys he always carried on his trouser belt, he unlocked the heavy cellar door, switched on the light and gestured to his prey who meekly stepped into his lair. He followed her in and silently shut the door behind them. Was he really doing this? As easily as he had dismissed Mrs Cappott? He hadn't planned or prepared either act other than in his fantasies yet this was the perfect time. It had been handed to him on a plate, was meant to be. How could it go wrong? He knew now after firing the housekeeper that he was all powerful, invincible. He felt strong, Godlike and indestructible. Anything for him was now possible. Anything. Everything.

Sara completed her descent and allowed her eyes to travel over the neat racks of dusted bottles. Before she knew what was happening or had chance to make a sound, the man she thought had become her confidante, her saviour even, had whipped the pashmina from her thin shoulders and wrapped it tightly around her face. She gasped; legs and arms flailing, trying to make sense of what she was experiencing.

He thought rapidly. Within seconds her belt was tying her skeletal wrists together and then to a rack. He checked she was safely silenced and secured before racing deftly up the steps and to the lounge where he collected her bag from the sofa. Retrieving, silencing and pocketing her iPhone, though he knew there was no signal beneath the house, he strode back to the make-shift prison, threw her bag into the depths, softly closed the weighty door and lent in the freezing porch with his back against its solidity, breathing for the first time in what seemed like minutes. He took a moment to stabilise his heart rate before walking calmly back through the porch door and carefully shutting it behind him before walking back into the hall where he found that Hugo thankfully was still nowhere to be seen. He opened the front door noisily and then slammed it. Hard. He had just slipped back from the main hall into his own quarters as Hugo could be heard coming down the stairs and calling out for Sara.

Phase one complete...easy; it had actually been quite fun acting spontaneously for once. He became aware that Hugo's voice which had been calling Sara's name more and more frantically was now calling Rupert's. He strolled out into the hall enquiringly.

"Have you seen Sara? I can't find her anywhere" Hugo's concerned voice had risen an octave.

"No, but I heard the front door slam, sir" he spoke in his usual, measured, slightly disapproving voice.

"It shook the whole house."

"Yes, I heard that too, but where on earth would she have gone?" he sounded somewhat calmer now that he had obtained at least some sort of an explanation.

"I really couldn't say, sir." This conversation was dragging. He needed to get back down to the cellar. The scarf and belt were only temporary and inefficient measures and he didn't want the annoying woman to work her way loose. Thank goodness there were two doors between them and the cellar just in case. Hugo was looking perplexed and worried.

"You could have a look along the street, maybe she's gone to the convenience store or even to the pharmacy near Sloane Avenue?" He ventured ingeniously, knowing that it would take a good fifteen minutes each way plus the questioning.

Hugo visibly relaxed and began to look like he might be prepared to wait till she reappeared. Damn.

"It's very cold and dark tonight though and no address in London is any place for a delicate young lady at this time." Rupert continued. Hugo looked immediately worried again.

"You're completely right of course, thank you for being so kind and caring about her." He said whilst grabbing the camel coat he'd worn every day since he'd got it.

"Ring me if she gets back before me, I've got my phone." he called as he shut the door behind him. Thank God for that. Rupert quickly fetched parcel tape, scissors, paper and pen from the study and was in the basement within moments.

Sara had heard Hugo calling her but his voice had sounded worryingly far away and muffled, the bloody cellar door must be a special thick safety one or something. Though she had tried and tried she knew her small voice, hidden as it was under layers of cashmere couldn't even penetrate two normal doors and she felt utterly confused and alone. She desperately tried to calm her mind so as to be able to clearly think her way out of this; she knew she could trust the logical brain she had been blessed with but had never tested it under such stressful conditions. She also knew that Rupert would be a challenging opponent; how could one win over someone with no empathy? No feelings? She had been correct about him all along but had been so shocked by his seeming compassion tonight and wrapped up in her desire to please Hugo that she had stupidly lost judgment. She couldn't begin to think what was actually going on in his head to do such a crazy thing but hoped she could somehow use his lack of rationality to her benefit. This very lack though, made him an exceptionally dangerous assailant. Frightened and at a severe disadvantage she may be, weak and defeat accepting she was not. The door had opened and he now stood before her, towering, exhibiting his strength. She searched his face, trying to lock onto his stare, challenging him defiantly with her eyes. He ignored her. She hid her fear, wanting rebelliously to show him how brave she was being, how strong. He wasn't interested. She was nothing. He didn't need to show his power, it was evident; it shone from him like an aura.

He just wished Hugo could see him now, be impressed by him, look up to him even but he understood that the mast...the mas...that Hugo wouldn't be ready to understand yet, wouldn't be ready to see that this was the right thing, see this act of kindness for what it was.

He quickly but neatly cut off a length of tape and held the scissors close to the face that was looking far too insolent and insubordinate. She flinched and started shaking involuntarily.

"You will make no sound" he stated simply in his bored voice, showing none of the amusement he felt at her predicament and carefully placed down the scissors. He saw her bright eyes dart to them and dull instantly as she correctly calculated that she was too helpless for them to be of any use to her. Deftly he pulled away the interim gag, smoothed the tape over her lips and wrapped it tightly around her head four times hating having to touch the loathsome skin and hair but accepting it as a necessity. Consoling himself with the knowledge it would soon be over he used another adhesive strip to fasten her ankles together.

"I'm now going to remove the belt from your wrists and you are going to write a letter to Hugo explaining that you have left and that you don't want to see him anymore. You are not going to be silly and struggle or try and hurt me because you will be punished for it. Do you understand?"

She nodded, hardly believing her luck at being able to send Hugo some sort of code and thinking quickly about how she could word it so as not alert her captor. This was her chance. He removed the belt and she rubbed her wrists together, surprised at how uncomfortable they had got in such a short length of time. She was going to have to toughen up, she admonished herself.

"No funny business" he said reading her mind and immediately feeling annoyed with himself for saying something so cheesy. He had no intentions of allowing any change in the dynamics of this exchange and moving his lips nearer to her ugly, pallid little face he enunciated each word as he whispered menacingly.
"Do. You. Understand?"
He was immensely proud of himself; whilst he hadn't planned it, the timing of the Cappott woman's dismissal was perfect. It would have been much more inconvenient having anyone else in the house. It was as though he were being told by some greater force, if one believed in such things that he were doing the right thing. He was acutely aware that he had not got unlimited time even though the love struck Hugo would be thorough in his search and be reluctant to come home till he had found Sara. What a silly wild goose chase he was on! He handed her the paper and parker. She stalled, continuing to rub her wrists.
"Do not irritate me" he threatened and something in his demeanour must have caused her to take his threat seriously because she took the pen and paper from him acquiescently.
"Write exactly what l say...and quickly."

Disappointment pierced through her like a knife; he was dictating! The glimpse of imagined freedom snuffed out like a candle and she felt something die inside her. She listened to him and numbly wrote.

Dear Hugo,

I'm truly sorry but I can't be with you any longer. I just don't love you enough to spend the rest of my life with you.

You are a lovely, lovely man and I know you will find happiness with someone else who can give you what you want.

Please do NOT try to contact or find me, this is my final decision.

Sara xxx

Rupert would of course never have used those ridiculous words but had seen enough films when Hugo had wanted company, which had featured Dear John letters. He paused, knowing he would find the next part particularly distasteful. She seemed to sense the slight change in him and stiffened as she braced herself for whatever he was planning. He was interested to note that her fear excited him and he realised he was no longer disliking this but in fact liking it very, very much indeed. It was a long time since he had felt so alive, so exhilarated, so in control, so aroused.

He freed the end of the tape from its roll, adhered it securely to the wine rack behind her and holding his breath so as not to have to smell her then deciding he actually wanted to breathe in her terror, circled it around her arms and body three and then four times, not wanting to stop, before wrapping it several times around the rack again. He sat back on his heels, somewhat uncomposed and flushed, and surveyed his handiwork; she was successfully restrained, helpless and vulnerable and he felt his blood pumping harder and harder through him until he felt that he would explode. He had been anxious about the enforced proximity of this exercise, thought it would have been too uncomfortable but whilst he had, of course, no desire for this woman, for any woman he had found the power he held over her nearly uncontainable. He glanced at her restraints one more time, hurried to the study to deposit the letter onto Hugo's desk, replaced the pen, tape and scissors and then made his way swiftly to his room lest he was tempted back to the cellar to lose control in a way he never had previously; he needed to be alone for this.

Chapter Ten

Thank God he was gone, at least for the time being. She admitted to herself that she was very frightened of the man but also found a moral high ground in finding him pathetic and disgusting which gave her a power of sorts. Even though she had seen the defects that Hugo was blind to, she hadn't ever foreseen just how depraved he could be. He was obviously sick in some way; she could swear he was actually getting off on being such a bully, the pervert! All her hopes lay with Hugo and she prayed that he would realise immediately that the preposterous letter hadn't been written willingly by her and that, in any case, she would never voluntarily leave him when they were so desperately and demonstrably happy. Surely he knew her well enough to see that she would never be so cowardly as to write such a letter rather than own her decision and discuss any possible issues face to face. Material possessions seemed meaningless now but under normal circumstances he must know that she would never leave all her pretty clothes, even her case was still upstairs. The whole idea of her leaving him now was absurd and she was certain he'd see that too and also pick up on the meagre number of kisses Rupert had sent because he knew she always sent him loads. She felt reasonably positive but whilst Hugo was an unusually sensitive and loving man, he was still a man and nowhere near as perceptive as her few female friends. If ever she had needed him to be intuitive rather than literal, it was now; she hoped she was being melodramatic when she wondered if her life might actually depend on it.

Having recovered his composure and feeling much calmer from the release, Rupert managed by the skin of his teeth to be waiting in the hall, looking what he hoped was suitably concerned when Hugo arrived home. It had not panned out like he could have expected but nevertheless phase two was complete and though he thought it himself, he was a genius!

"Any news??" Hugo bellowed fretfully before he was even fully through the door, "I've shown everyone I could in the entire area her picture on my phone and been in all the shops and restaurants all the way up past Sloane Avenue and no one has seen her! This is a nightmare, a complete nightmare. I just can't think where she could have gone. We were going to have cuddles when I finished my call! Was I too long? Did she get cross with me? Cross enough to leave? Maybe it's some sort of joke? Could it be a joke?

Could she be hiding?" he wound down pathetically.

"I don't know, but I can see you're not finding it particularly amusing. It certainly seems strange, I agree, but you've always said that women are temperamental" Rupert answered.

It was true; Hugo had always said that but Rupert also knew that his employer wasn't feeling like this was a trivial moodiness or funny in any way. He was clearly very agitated but he was bound to calm down soon when he realised she wasn't coming back and it was a fait accompli. This not knowing would be the worst part.

The demented man rushed through the house searching each room before moving onto the next. It interested Rupert that this activity wasn't unlike his own much calmer and more methodical searching for and eradicating any possibility of pending horrors. He listened, for quite some time, to the unholy and evermore haphazard clattering and accompanying shouting of Sara's name with quiet amusement until the house fell silent. Sauntering into the hall, he found Hugo standing before the rear porch door, shoulders heaving, fists clenching and unclenching, clearly fighting his inner demons and stealing himself to enter the part of the house his phobia had never let him close to. Rupert hadn't considered that Hugo's feelings for Sara could possibly conquer his incapacitating fears of small spaces and shook his head at the extent of his indoctrinisation. If only the silly man had known how very close he was to saving his even sillier girlfriend! The childhood game of hotter and colder came mischievously to his mind. Not allowing his thoughts to slow his efficiency, Rupert spoke calmly.

"Please sir, let me search the cellars for you, you've done enough. It's very cramped down there and I know you won't like it."

Hugo allowed himself to be guided back into the body of the hall and look on forlornly as his assistant helped him.

After unlocking the cellar door, Rupert stood listening to the pathetically quiet moanings escaping the taped lips for an annoying but appropriate time before locking it once again and making his way back to Hugo.

"Nothing sir, sorry." Hugo continued to stand motionless, the two of them held in a surreal tableau, before bursting into renewed chaotic, disturbed and even less productive searching until suddenly, from the study, he let out an almost inhuman howl. He had found it at last then.

The distraught man flew into the hall brandishing the only link he currently held to what he still, pathetically, thought of as his cherished Sara and, to Rupert's dismay, dropped his head and shoulders and started to sob. The appalled personal assistant was at a complete loss about what might be expected of him. Was he supposed to offer comfort? Place a supporting hand on the heaving back? Fortunately the dilemma was taken from him as Hugo turned and galloped upstairs, slamming a door behind him.

Hugo ran to his bathroom and threw up into the toilet. He felt sick and numb and yet somehow through the numbness a pain like no other pierced him like a blade. His gut wrenched at the horrific mutation of the experiences he'd had two weeks earlier when Sara had been poorly and he had utterly and inappropriately panicked at not being able to contact her. It was as though his former suffering had been a cruel practice for this nightmare and he was being mocked for being so senseless and over the top; this million times magnification and grotesque augmentation were his retribution. He had cried wolf once too many times and through that idiocy he had driven away the only woman he had ever loved. He wretched from his now empty stomach and in his crouched pose, cradled his head in his hands and started to rock. His loss was all consuming. He hadn't just lost her; she had been his future and he had lost his future. She had been his life and his life now had no meaning. There was only one person in the world to whom he wanted to turn for comfort and she was no longer his. He shuffled to his bedroom and lay motionless, alone and utterly despondent.

Chapter Eleven

Sara had heard Hugo calling her name again, his voice seeming, though scarcely audible, to get closer and closer and when the cellar door had opened, she'd dared to believe he had come to rescue her but despite her loudest cries to him, somehow he hadn't found her and the door had closed again. She still couldn't understand what had happened. She had been sure their love could overcome any hurdle but her poor angel's phobia added to his understandable anxiety around having lost her must have been too paralysing. She was hurt and angry and lonely and confused but she was not prepared to be beaten.

....

She was used to being hungry; had long since learned to reframe the discomfort of the rumbling with the slightly uncomfortable but necessary munching of her fat by the stomach monster. She had even got used to and now actually embraced the spacey feeling, welcoming it as a sign that she was both in control and getting slimmer. But now her abdomen ached with more than usual hunger and she was desperately thirsty. Though she couldn't see it in the darkness she knew she was surrounded by wine and not being able to reach the liquid, albeit alcoholic, was almost worse than it not being there; so near and yet so hopelessly far. She had no way of knowing what time it was; it had been oppressively dark at all times apart from when Rupert had briefly snapped on the light to tape her up. Whilst being bound, she'd seen a door that must lead to the part of the cellar at the front of the house and fervently wished she was in that room. That must be where the window was that she had seen from outside. Incarcerated in this dungeon she craved natural light, traffic and pedestrian noise and most importantly, a way of attracting attention. Not only was she bereft of those lifelines but was also under the part of the house never used during the cold months. The blackness of her cell created a sensation of isolation, bewilderment and disorientation yet she knew she must get the tape off her face and try to make herself heard. Damn him for not just sticking it to her skin so she could have easily manipulated it off; tape stuck to tape couldn't be budged but she started working her jaw, trying to crease the tape into a thinner band. Her face ached and her skin burned but it was taking her mind away from the hunger and dehydration induced twisting pain in her tummy, the throbbing in her head, the chaffing of the restraints and the muscle burn caused by her awkward position.

. . . .

The light headedness and beginnings of visual disturbances were reminiscent of her recent flu virus but she knew the symptoms now were simply due to lack of sustenance. Being somewhat malnourished after her virus meant that she had very few resources. She chastised herself for not having had a drink when she'd arrived or even on the train. She knew she was supposed to have a couple of litres of water a day but often forgot. When she had first been learning not to eat she had used water to fill herself up but once her body had grown accustomed to the low calorie regime she had become really lazy about it. She shook herself impatiently; she was not going down either the path of self blame or self pity and she was going to stay focused. She tried to fathom why he was keeping her here and was beginning to fear that he may be crazy enough for anything. She didn't want t to think in this way but felt it would help if she understood; surely, if he had wanted her dead, he'd have struck her or something straight away. She felt she needed to know why she was being held and how long he intended to keep her fastened here. Could he possibly have become so unhinged, so psychotic that he was intending to leave her here to die or had simply forgotten about her? What other explanations could there be? Could he be punishing her for some reason? Punishing Hugo? For what and to what end?

She continued working her jaw and pushing out her tongue with renewed strength and determination to free herself of the sticky gag and finally, gasping, she released it from her lips so that it was just a tight thong across her mouth. It bit into the corners of her mouth but at least, thank God, she could now call for help and call she did. And shout and scream and screech and yell until her throat was stinging and raw and her head felt like it was shattering. Was there anybody even there to hear? Did she have to accept, fatalistically, that just as very little sound penetrated her tomb, very little sound escaped to the world outside? The odds against her were growing heavier. She couldn't differentiate if it was due to exhaustion, dehydration, lack of oxygen from shouting or her rising panic but she could feel her heart beat quickening, her reasoning slowing and her strength of resolve fading. She must stay calm and clear minded; she forced herself to think.

Sara thought of Hugo. She was, altruistically, almost more worried for her sweetheart than she was for herself she would give anything to hold and comfort him right now. She wanted to reassure him even more than she needed that reassurance herself. As he hadn't come to find her, she reasoned, he must truly believe she had actually left him and be out of his mind with worry and pain but she desperately needed him to start thinking clearly... and fast.

. . . .

She felt dizzy and confused and lost. She searched her inner resources and discovered a memory of her yoga teacher telling her gently to breathe in pink...to breathe in love...so she breathed in the delicate pink of her cashmere jumper as she visualised its colour in the darkness...she breathed it in..breathed in the love that Hugo had felt when he'd first seen her try it on....inhaled love..peace..purity... and then, as instructed, she exhaled negativity...ugliness...perversion...pain ...hatred....loathing...cruelty...death..

This was not working! She had done a damn good job, she told herself, of being positive and calm and brave and rational but her wrists where they had rubbed and chaffed against the tape were bleeding sticky blood onto her hands, her whole body ached agonisingly and she felt exhausted and sick. But she was not a fucking victim; she was furious, incandescently furious! Why the hell was this happening? How could that bastard have done this? Been so cruel? So inhuman? Did he really think that dehydration was a gentle slipping away? Did he even give a shit? She hated him like she had never hated anybody before. She hated him so badly that the rawness of it wanted to burst from her like a

76

volcanic eruption...like she would to explode with rage. She wanted to get hold of the vile pervert and vent her all consuming rage on him. She wanted to hurt him like he was hurting her. She wanted to kill him. But she was tied here...she was helpless...she was impotent... She bowed her head and she wept.

....

Rupert wondered, analytically, what his next action should be. It had been very different last time; simply administrating an overdose with tablets his mother had been prescribed to a woman who often struggled knowing who she was, let alone how many pills she had taken that day had been the easiest thing in the world. Maybe he should have chosen a time when she was more deranged but, everyone knew she could flip at any given moment and he'd rather liked making it slightly more challenging. No one would have even questioned her passing had she not spoken to her psychiatrist only that week and had been reported as being more lucid than she had for several sessions. It had been sheer bad luck that the stupid jobsworth had felt it necessary to take that information to the authority's attention and the matter had needed to be investigated.

Still, after an autopsy, an inquest and a ridiculous amount of questioning by the local plod, the death had been recorded as an accidental overdose. The administering of her medication had not required any particular planning and he had felt somewhat cheated and resentful that it had been so effortless and unchallenging. Even the police questioning had been yawningly undemanding; as he had felt neither remorse nor guilt, he hadn't had to hide anything. The only slight task had been pretending to be the distraught and bereaved son but providentially, his natural withdrawn nature, reserve and introversion were fortuitously construed as grief.

Certainly he had wanted Sara to be removed and had even had some vague thoughts of facilitating that removal but hadn't yet started enjoying the planning thereof with any real seriousness. It had been his pure good fortune that Sara had chosen that precise time, when Hugo was otherwise engaged and Rupert had decided to speak to her for completely unrelated reasons to give him the perfect opportunity on a plate, so to speak. He had seized the moment; his actions had been wholly opportunist and there had been very little time to think yet he had been able to demonstrate very considerable skills. Parts of the operation had shocked him, he flushed recalling his exhilaration but he had proved beyond doubt that if he could succeed with no planning, he could achieve anything he set his mind to. It was a very favourable sensation but was nonetheless tinged with more than a little disappointment that he still hadn't had the anticipation of preparing thoroughly.

Rupert had not been in the cellar since he had rather lost his composure. Once or twice his curiosity had nearly taken him down there but, even though her gag would have stopped her being able to annoy him with her stupid squeaky voice, he would still have had to stomach her poppy out elfin eyes; imploring and pleading were such unattractive qualities. Other than interest what other possible reason was there for him to go down there? Now in calm thought, he felt self disgust at his temporary lapse and found the idea of the intimacy associated with physical contact too abhorrent to even consider touching her again. So strangling was out. Nor did he relish the idea of using any type of weapon he could think of. He could poison her, of course, but the idea of simply leaving her there to degenerate interested and satisfied him most. He mused on these various possibilities with less involvement than most people would have decided whether to have potato or rice as an accompaniment to their meal.

Rupert hadn't spoken to Hugo today. During the period between yesterday and this evening he had occasionally mounted the stairs to Hugo's room and listening carefully had heard the red head weeping pathetically. There had been one time this morning when he had surfaced briefly, blotchy faced and tear stained but Rupert had purposefully avoided him. Under usual circumstances he would have liked to have had his employer all to himself for a day but this day he was rather revolted by the feebleness being exhibited by the lesser man and preferred to wait till sense had been seen.

Chapter Twelve

Sometimes she felt like she was floating...drifting.... her altered consciousness was aware of pain ebbing and flowing through her body...enveloping her...possessing her... but it seemed somehow to be slightly disconnected...separate from her.. Even in her semi delirium she understood that her situation was dire and though she could not be sure how long she'd been there she thought more than forty-eight hours. In a lucid time she calculated that whilst she was using extremely little energy and the atmosphere was fairly cool and constant, given her current health and reserves, she couldn't realistically expect to live without food or water for more than a total of five days. She forced her straying mind to stay awake and logical; she must try and think her way to safety. She wasn't strong enough to break the tape he'd used so someone needed to come and free her. Maggie and Lucy wouldn't think of contacting her now that they were on their Christmas break except for maybe a text on New Year's Eve which they wouldn't even necessarily expect a reply to. They would understandably assume she was being happily romantic with Hugo for a month.

Charlotte and Emily were lovely but not established enough friends to contact her when they were wrapped up with their own families and again, wouldn't necessarily expect a reply if they did message her. Her Exeter friends wouldn't know anything was wrong until uni restarted in January. Her parents were expecting her on Boxing Day but that must be well over a week away....what day must it be now?... and there was no one else. She'd never really thought of herself as a loner, rather an independent and resourceful young woman but now she wished she had been more gregarious.

When she had ever thought of a 'Billy-no-mates' type of character, it had been about people like Rupert; the idea of having anything in common with him was mind numbingly horrific.

She felt more alone than she had in her entire life. She had had so much to look forward to as Hugo's wife with more fun, holidays and money to spend than she had ever thought possible. Her dream was fading away from her reality; that evil monster was stealing it from her. In less than two weeks she had been going to the country estate in Dorset for Christmas, was there any way that could still happen? Any way she could still escape this hell? Or, if Rupert didn't let her go, at least maybe he would give her a little water and food every few days? Was that the best she could possibly hope for now? Was he intending to keep her here over Christmas? Would Hugo still go to Dorset without her? Of course he would want the comfort of his family after his girlfriend had 'left him'; he would be thinking of rebuilding his life without her. She thought of herself, lying her in agony, kept barely alive with sips of water and crumbs whilst the monster sat alone upstairs at the head of Hugo's elegant huge yew dining table with a turkey dinner for one and a single cracker and felt like she was going to vomit. Angrily, furiously, she pulled on her restraints again but the tape had no stretch in it and wasn't giving at all. She strained harder...and harder... her attempts becoming more and more frenzied until she gave up, in a flood of frustrated and hopeless tears.

....

Hugo was searching his tattered memories for the hundredth time. He still didn't know how he had achieved it but he must have *really* upset Sara for her to walk out on him so finally and abruptly. She had seemed as happy as he but maybe she just been pretending to be happy, for some reason, when she had arrived for Christmas. He knew he should have been much more supportive of her finding new friends rather than showing jealousy. He cursed himself for having kept calling her that day; she was a grown woman for God's sake and he should have respected her space. He was excruciatingly ashamed of how pathetically desperate and needy he must have appeared. He should never have allowed her to see such deplorable traits; if he couldn't have altered how he had felt then, at least, he should have had the sense to hide it. And that was, of course, the problem; he had very little sense. It was little wonder that she no longer wanted to be with him. He had always known he wasn't good enough for her and now that she had her new clever friends he could completely understand that he was surplus to requirements. She had seemed so loving when she'd arrived what seemed like years ago and was in actuality only a day. He could see how the phone call could have easily been the straw that broke the proverbial camel's back. It must have seemed so terribly rude when she had only just arrived and hadn't seen him for a week. What an idiot he was! He should have ignored the damn call; it had been nowhere near as important as her. And now he'd lost her. Had she actually been thinking of leaving him for some time? Planning it? Had they been living a lie? He winced. He had been holding onto all the lovely romantic things she had said to him but maybe they had just been empty and meaningless. She must have been extremely angry with him to only send three kisses. That had been such a slap in the face and even worse than no kisses really when she had always sent him gazillions. She must completely despise him not to even want the clothes and perfumes he'd bought her.

From the depth of despair, he suddenly salvaged an inner strength and realised that he couldn't just leave it like this, couldn't just let her walk out of his life; he loved her enough for both of them and wasn't prepared to give her up without a fight. He needed to find her, make her see he was worth another chance and win her back. He just wished he knew how. Whilst he hadn't wanted to appear like the needy man she must have found suffocating and had driven her away, he had already left several messages pleading with her to come back to him. He hadn't felt up to talking to anyone and knew he would only both embarrass himself and worry other people but had texted Maggie. In order to sound less dramatic he had fabricated a story about them having got their wires crossed and become separated whilst shopping. He had postulated that she may have lost her phone. He knew the story would hold no water under scrutiny but had been beyond desperate. Maggie had messaged back to say that she had not heard from her, that she was certain they'd be reunited very shortly and to have a wonderful Christmas. Escalating his search he took a deep breath and called Sara's mother to no further avail. The blade he had felt within him since he'd discovered her farewell letter twisted a little further and he was utterly deflated.

....

After a comfortable and satisfying night's sleep, Rupert heard Hugo blundering down the stairs. He hoped that he too had slept well, be more settled and that the healing process was underway. He was just about to ignore the noisy decent and venture out with a cheery greeting when he heard the chink of what he could only assume was the brandy decanter against a heavy lead crystal glass. These were kept on a silver tray on the side board in the dining room and, to his knowledge, had never been touched by Hugo until this week. The liquid level had never changed other than on the few occasions that brandy drinkers had visited. Another clink, followed by several expletives could be heard; clearly this was still not the time to approach him. Rupert shook his head disappointedly and retired back to his own sitting room. What was the man playing at? This was not a respectable way for a gentleman to conduct himself. Hugo had always been so calm, placid and stable. These had been some of his most endearing qualities and yet now he was behaving like a buffoon. He was becoming a mess and worse, he was becoming a joke. Rupert sighed, not wanting to lose either faith, patience or respect for the man he had looked up to as the 'master' for all these years but needed him to start showing some back bone and decorum fairly swiftly.

Hugo had shuddered violently after downing his first glass of amber fluid; Christ, did people actually enjoy that stuff? He gulped down another and shuddered less as a very welcome warm numbness flowed through his aching body and mind. The continual and haunting questions that had been hurtling around his head for two days, eradicating any chance of coherent thought, let alone sleep, slowed their scurrying to a manageable speed. Being no type of drinker, he felt noticeably inebriated, yet he observed he could concentrate better than he had latterly. He had felt drunk from lack of sleep but it hadn't taken the edge of the pain that this did; he could now appreciate why people became dependent on alcohol.

Two heads were better than one, he decided, especially when one of them was his, he thought wryly; he must meet Jonathan. He dragged on his hat and coat, burst into the outside world and phoned his friend, taking several attempts to negotiate the numbers. It rang four times..five..before he heard the ring silence. Before his friend could answer he blurted,

"I know it's only Sunday but can we meet?"

Jonathan had just sat down with Jane in a coffee shop and the last thing he wanted was this strange slurring Hugo getting in his way when he had worked so hard trying to 'casually' arrange a platonic meeting. However, not only was Hugo's request completely unprecedented but he'd also never known him to sip more than one glass of anything; this must be important.

"Of course, I'm in the coffee shop I like on the Kings Road, with, er, Jane, why don't you join us."

Despite everything Hugo still understood the implications of what his friend was saying and was still polite enough to check if that was really ok. Jonathan assured him that it was and twenty minutes later Hugo was taking a seat opposite the pair as if he were being interviewed by a panel. The walk and fresh air had sobered him up enough to be coherent but not so much that the debilitating whirlwind of thoughts had restarted to paralyse him. He described to them, best he could, the events of the last few days and they listened intently in horrified silence.

His narrative ground to a halt and he became aware of his surroundings for the first time. He looked hopelessly around searching, as if it might be here that he would find the answers he craved; bizarrely, for a moment he thought he had. He darted unsteadily to the far end of the cafe, knocking a chair over in his haste and scattering the contents of a lady's bag as he knocked it off a neighbouring table. He slammed to an expectant and excited halt in front of a blonde lady who was adding milk to her mug of coffee. The flurry of activity caused the surprised woman to look up at him, slightly alarmed and gather her two children tightly to her. How could he have thought this middle aged woman could have been his beautiful Sara? What was wrong with him? He mumbled an apology to her, the woman who was collecting up her belongings and the room in general before retreating embarrassed to his table where he apologised again.

Jonathan, who had known Sara for some time and fairly well, was dumbfounded that she could have left in any, let alone, this manner. Jane sat silently, her fingers steepled beneath her chin. Hugo studied her. He'd only met her once before at his party when he had only had eyes for Sara who had been nearby, schmoozing the crowd. Now he could see why his friend was so besotted; whilst she was of course not a patch on Sara she was, nevertheless, a strikingly beautiful woman. Long, dark, shiny hair framed an intelligent face with a good bone structure, fine features, natural pout and flawless skin. Her long fingers with their perfectly manicured nails slowly beat a rhythm in front of her long pale neck. Hugo felt as if he had not breathed while he had waited for her reaction and as she shook her luxuriant mane and placed her hands on the table by her now almost empty earthenware mug, he exhaled audibly.

"From what you have told us, not only was there no reason for Sara to leave you but every reason for her to stay and yet she has gone, without the clothes she keeps at your house and you have a farewell letter from her"

Hugo seemed to shrink as he nodded.

"You're absolutely sure it's her writing?" she checked.

He nodded again.

"And you showed her picture to everyone on the square?"

"Yes, I searched the whole house, the square and well beyond" he confirmed.

"What about taxi firms? We need to find where she went"

"No" Hugo admitted, "I did ask Rupert though and he didn't hear anything except the door slamming. It's so awful to think we were living a lie and she was just playing me somehow"

"Hugo," she said soothingly, "I don't think you're thinking productively. What I would like to do, if you don't mind, is to call round some cab firms and for you to go home, properly sober up and try to rest best you can . Then, in the morning I'd really like to do some gentle hypnosis with you to help you find some clarity. Do you think we could do that?"

"I use Kensington Car Services, I have a contract with them" the distraught and intoxicated man said numbly in monotone,

"I haven't been hypnotised before and I don't love the idea, do you really think it could help?"

He spoke much more candidly than he would normally.

"It's very relaxing and Jane's really good at it" Jonathan enthused, covering any awkwardness "it can't do any harm can it?" he said coaxingly.

"What exactly does it entail? I feel a bit uncomfortable about being out of control...but I'll do anything, anything to find Sara and win her back."

"I promise there's absolutely nothing to worry about" the reassuring professional kicked in,

"You will be in control the whole time and will be able to remember everything that is said. You will even be able to move, open your eyes or talk if you want to but I'm sure it will feel too peaceful and safe. All I'll do is relax your body and conscious mind by talking softly to you and then talk directly to your subconscious mind, which always has your best interests at heart. I won't ask you to talk and all you'll have to do is rest. You won't even have to listen to me if you don't want to because your subconscious mind will hear and understand everything I have to say anyway. After a few minutes I'll bring you back to full consciousness and you'll feel more refreshed and clear than you have in days so that we can move rationally forward. How does that sound?"

Hugo had begun to feel a little calmer, something about the timbre of her voice made him feel less anxious and he thought that maybe he could start to trust her. She was probably a good hypnotherapist; his best friend said so and he could hear that her voice was very soothing. Suddenly he began to panic and suspected that he was being hoodwinked in some way by the two people he thought he trusted. Was his mind playing tricks on him? Was he being paranoid?

"Are you hypnotising me now?" He probed suspiciously.

"No," she smiled, hiding her discomfort at being accused of unethical behaviour. She reminded herself that Hugo wasn't himself at the moment and in any case, wouldn't know about the moral principles of therapy. "I would never do that without your authority, that wouldn't be the right way to gain your trust, would it? But I suppose I was just starting to try and relax you a bit, I hope that's ok?"

"Ok" he mumbled acquiescingly, "I'm sorry." He realised that he had probably accused her of something wrong but was much too wrapped up in his loss and confusion to worry about it over much. He knew though that he definitely didn't want to upset someone who was trying to help him or alienate his good friend. Even if he were to trust her not to embarrass him, he really couldn't believe it would be successful but wasn't about to be further churlish by admitting his scepticism. If there was any chance at all of its usefulness, he was prepared to take it. Her voice gently interrupted his thoughts.

"Now, go home and try to rest, there's nothing more you can do tonight. I'd like you, please, to be thinking about what sort of place you would feel most peaceful in, a beach or a forest maybe. It can be real or imagined as long as it makes you feel nice and calm. Tomorrow I'll ask you to describe it to me so I can use it as a relaxing safe place in your hypnotherapy." she smiled comfortingly. He didn't really understand but he resolved to think about it because like Jonathan said, what harm could it do?

They made their goodbyes, checked that Hugo was safe to get home by himself and arranged that he would be at her consultation room at ten the following day, Monday.

Chapter Thirteen

Her mouth was parched. She tried to lick her sore, dry lips but her swollen tongue was almost too dry to escape her mouth. Her lips felt cracked and caked with something and the plastic tape cut into her face. She felt dreadfully nauseas and her mouth tasted terrible. Her body heaved but there was nothing left to vomit. She'd completely emptied the contents of her stomach, basically a packet of air popped corn the first two times she'd been sick. It must be coating the front of the sweater she'd liked so much. For the first time she praised the darkness that enveloped her for saving her the full horror of seeing it. The full degradation. The full humiliation. If she couldn't see the regurgitated mess she could certainly taste it...mixed with salty and metallic blood.

She had never felt so ill. She ached all over and her eyes and inside her nostrils stung. She couldn't understand why Maggie hadn't been in today. She desperately needed a glass of water and wanted her phone from her bag at the bottom of the bed but felt too weak to reach it. Her legs and even arms were cramping horribly, her flu must be getting worse. Her feet and hands were freezing even though she was so wrapped up in the duvet that she couldn't move her arms. She drew her knees up sharply to her chest in agony as her stomach felt like it was exploding with pain. It must be overcast because there was no light coming from the moon; it was always so much worse being ill at night. Through the darkness she could somehow make out Hugo walking toward her. Thank God! She'd known he wouldn't let her down. He seemed to be with someone but then she realised it wasn't a person but rather that he was carrying an enormous human sized teddy bear holding a pink heart with an H on it. There were other people behind though though...oddly, when she didn't think they had ever met him, it was her grandparents ...how lovely but how silly of her to have got confused and thought they had passed away. Behind them she could see a tiny sliver of light as a door opened a chink...

Chapter Fourteen

Hugo managed to dodge his personal assistant, hearing his footsteps as he shut the front door and escaped into the fresh air. He wasn't up to talking, let alone to Rupert who he felt sure would ridicule the idea of hypnosis and he didn't feel up to that disdainful and weary look today. He still had hardly slept, was feeling fragile, had what he assumed was a hangover and was more than a little nervous about his impending therapy. He had only just left the Square when he saw her. It was definitely Sara this time, wearing a scarlet hat and cape which must be new but it was certainly her. Her gossamer hair flowed over her shoulders and back. He hastened his step, broke into a run. The relief, the joy, the anticipation, the love! It wasn't her.

Rupert, very uncharacteristically, didn't particularly feel like working. As there was unlikely to be anything of importance on the market so close to Christmas and Hugo being obviously unconcerned about the business, having left the house without an explanation, he decided for the first time ever to give himself the day off.

Hugo was still rattled about finding and losing Sara when he arrived at the address Jane had given him. He hadn't actually known what to expect but had vaguely thought of swinging pocket watches, people enjoying eating onions or acting like chicken and maybe cabinets of paraphernalia and a rug covered chaise longue like the one he'd seen in a photograph of the Sigmund Freud museum. Seconds after he had rung the door bell, Jane welcomed him warmly into her conventional, nicely decorated extension and gently but swiftly deposited the jet black cat which had followed her out of the main body of the house back through the door, closing it gently behind her.

"Sorry about Ninja, she's so nosy and sneaky and can't bear to miss a thing. How are you this morning? Please, take a seat." She gestured toward two deep purple corduroy chairs and a low glass table on which stood two glasses of iced and limed water. He chose the one with its back to the wall, sat down and surveyed the room warily. There was another, similar but pale green chair along with what looked like an Ikea armchair and footstool in ivory leather in the corner of the room. An enormous ornate guilt framed mirror nearly filled the far end wall cleverly doubling the actual size of the room. There were several tasteful pictures and ornaments in the green and aubergine of the chairs and a large cozy thick piled woolen rug in pale cream over broad pale oak floorboards. The room was furnished quite differently from how he would have expected from their limited meetings. Her simple and classical style of dress contrasted with her approach to interior design which was modern, experimental, avant-garde even. He had to admit he felt fairly comfortable in this room but scanned it analytically to see if there was anything out of the ordinary to distrust. The only possible thing he could pick up on was an ivory cube of tissues on the coffee table. As he had in truth spent a good part of the last three and a half days close to or in tears, he found that the box's contents were actually a welcome sight rather than intimidating.

Jane started by apologetically reporting that she had drawn a blank with the taxi firms but also informed him of the very positive news that when she had taken the liberty of phoning round the local hospitals, that had also yielded no results. They talked a little about the peaceful place she'd asked him to think about and he described to her a forest he had seen in a cartoon film as a child which had stayed with him because it had seemed almost magical in its beauty and tranquillity. His adult self thought it was probably juvenile and silly but it felt that the idyllic scene was just where he wanted to be right now. He told her about the forest glade with its tall trees and dappled light, the trickling, glistening stream, the tame woodland creatures, the soft undergrowth and the gnarled but comfortable wooden bench. He felt terribly foolish at first, especially when he told her about the rabbits and such like but Jane was so reassuring, so non judgemental, so warm that he was soon feeling much more at ease. Ten minutes later, when she asked him to move to the more comfortable leather chair and put his feet up, he did so happily and without demur. Yesterday he had almost given up, had been so locked in his misery and alcoholic haze that he feared he would never find his sweetheart but this wonderful 'marvel' of a woman was giving him fresh hope.

She took her place on the pistachio coloured chair and he settled into what, after several nights of very little sleep, looked extremely luxurious and inviting. In an even calmer way than usual, she invited him to close his eyes which he was very ready to do and methodically instructed him to relax every part of his body from the crown of his head to the tips of his toes. The cadence and tone of her voice seemed to carry him away to a place where he could easily access his special and relaxing forest glade. She offered him the opportunity to make any changes he might prefer so he carpeted the forest floor with soft springy green moss. Her voice talked to him of clarity, of strength, of confidence, of wisdom and introduced him to metaphors such as the morning mist clearing in the little forest giving him the clarity to see the trees and paths beyond. She talked to him about the clean, sparkling stream tumbling over the rocks and tree roots and how he could perfectly and clearly see the river bed. She then taught him how he could touch the thumb and index finger of his left hand together whenever he needed to feel as relaxed, resourced and clear as he did here in the forest glade. It all felt so real and lovely and just as she had promised that when it was time to come back he found that he was both refreshed and relaxed. He was also a firm advocate of hypnotherapy. Even if just used as a relaxation tool, he had never known one to beat it.

She handed him his tumbler of water and as he sipped he noticed how clear the water was and how clear he felt.

"Sara wouldn't have left me" he stated simply and then,

"We were both crazy about each other, it wasn't just me, I wasn't projecting my feelings. She truly loved me, we had been cuddling and kissing only minutes earlier." he looked down shyly "Wherever she has gone, it was not through choice. Either she was simply taken by force or somebody persuaded her to leave briefly and then prevented her return. Maybe they requested she look at something outside and then bungled her into a car or something. No not the former, there was no noise, no sign of a struggle. Oh my God, my baby's been kidnapped, poor angel!"

After a pause where Jane remained silent to let him think, he looked up with dawning horror. "As much as I like the idea that I could immediately and easily make this nightmare disappear with some cash, I would have received a ransom demand by now if that was how it happened. She must have been taken but not kidnapped." Jane sat quietly and allowed the process to take place. He took the now crumpled note from his pocket and with new eyes, reread it.

Dear Hugo,
I'm truly sorry but I can't be with you any longer. I just don't love you enough to spend the rest of my life with you.
You are a lovely, lovely man and I know you will find happiness with someone else who can give you what you want.
Please do NOT try to contact or find me, this is my final decision.
Sara xxx

He refused to believe that only minutes after they'd been so loving, she could have written those words of her own volition. He had thought that she was so cross with him that she had only used three kisses and left all her things in the bedroom but, now with a clearer head he could see it just too far out of character to be plausible.

With greater clarity than he could ever remember experiencing, he talked his thoughts through with Jane who was really pleased that she had facilitated his focussing. He explained that he now clearly saw that Sara had been taken against her will and must have been forced to write the letter. However, it didn't appear to be a kidnapping and he still had no idea why on earth she had been abducted or by whom. His task had to be to work out who had seized her. It was Monday, his day to meet Jonathan so he and Jane decided to continue their conversation in the restaurant so that the three of them could work it out. Having already achieved so much he felt very confident that with their combined skills they would sort this out, Sara would come back and he would buy her as many puppies of any colour and breed as she wanted!

When Jane and Hugo arrived Jonathan was, as usual, already at their table. Though acutely aware this wasn't a social meeting, he struggled to contain his pleasure at seeing his belle and fought his beam to a small smile as he stood up to greet them. He shook his friend's hand and then, with a hint of a blush, he kissed Jane on both cheeks. The two men had never had a companion to join them for this established lunch meeting but today was a very necessary exception and this particular companion was very welcome to both of them for their different reasons.

Jonathan waited very patiently for both of them to settle into their seats and their drinks to be ordered and brought over before enquiring eagerly about the hypnotherapy success. Hugo reiterated everything that he had become clear on, prompted occasionally by Jane and when he had finished the three of them sat in silence for a moment whilst Jonathan assimilated the information.

"Well..." pondered Jonathan, now up to speed "It seems then, as there was no evidence of breaking and entry, that she could only have been taken by someone who came to the door or someone who phoned or texted asking her to go to the door."

"But neither Rupert nor I heard the doorbell or knock on the door...maybe there could have been a very quiet knock...or a pebble or something thrown at the window?"

"But why would anyone want to do any of those things and were could they have taken her?" he whispered plaintively. "What reason could there be? There is nobody I can possibly imagine that would do this. No jealous ex-lovers, no wounded friends or business acquaintances. Sara kept herself to herself and every one with whom she did come into contact loved her to bits. How could they not?" his voice had been steadily raising and feeling himself start to freeze with anxiety he pressed his left thumb and first finger together. Immediately he felt the stress start to drain away and turned to Jane with excitement and surprise but she had already seen and was nodding approvingly at him with a kind, proud smile.

Jacques came over and sensing instantly that their manner was far more sombre than usual, quietly took their food order. Jane, who wasn't accustomed to French cuisine, asked the boys to order for her which they did efficiently without needing to see the menu.

She started to speak quietly.

"Look, I, erm, don't want to speak entirely out of turn here, but aren't we all completely overlooking Rupert?"

"Rupert?!" both men chorused incredulously.

"Think about it. He was alone with her so had the opportunity. He could possibly even have had the help of an accomplice or maybe paid the person who took her. You've admitted he and Sara weren't exactly the closest of friends."

"I know," spluttered Hugo, "but this? Why on earth would he? You don't even know him! I do and I'm certain you're barking up the wrong tree. That man's been indispensable! And as for an accomplice! This is utter nonsense."

"I'm sorry, I really don't want to upset you but it's precisely because you know him so well that you're finding it hard to believe." she continued in her soft reassuring voice, "I could be completely wrong of course and hope I am. I admit I have no idea how or why he could have planned it but I just think we should be examining every possibility."

The two men sat silently struggling with her suggestion but whilst Jane felt guilty about distressing Hugo, she had learned not to ignore her intuitions; her gut feelings didn't usually let her down. At that moment their meal arrived and was served professionally and quietly affording a little time for the therapist's idea to sink in.

When Jacques had left the table, she said.

"You're right, I don't know Rupert. Would you mind telling me some more about him?" And when he didn't answer,

"How did you two meet? I think Jonathan said you went way back?"

Hugo squeezed his finger and thumb together. "I suppose we really got to know each other at university when we shared a house and he was already working for me but actually we met as teens when his late mother cleaned for us. She used to bring him along with her when I was home from school one summer holiday. The poor woman died only a few weeks after that. Dreadful story, his father committed suicide later the same week. So tragic."

"How dreadful" gasped Jane, visibly shocked. Jonathan too had never heard this. After a pause, he managed.

"I didn't know that and I think it might be really significant." Jonathan's innate instincts were kicking in too and he glanced at Jane who was nodding in agreement and looking noticeably paler.

"Rupert understandably doesn't like to talk about it or for it to be known and discussed. He doesn't want sympathy, he said. I always respected those wishes and I don't ever think about it myself to be honest."

"But can't you see it could be important now?" Jane spoke in gentle, though grave tones.
Hugo looked perplexed.

"I hardly see that an accidental overdose by a very troubled woman and a suicidal drowning of a grieving husband could have any bearing on Sara's disappearance. Aren't you both clutching at straws..and quite frankly wasting time? I know Rupert much better than either of you and this is insultingly preposterous! Do you not think I would know if he was capable of stealing away my Sara and sending her God knows where?!" He spoke more angrily than he had meant to and lowered his eyes to avoid seeing their reaction.

The three sat in silence for a few moments, none of them wanting to escalate the argument, all of them wanting to move forward. Jane looked empathically at Hugo, understanding his sadness and pain, reaching out figuratively and physically she gently touched his hand. He felt her compassion and remembered that she had told him hypnotherapy wasn't a magic wand and he had to work toward staying clear headed. He pressed his thumb and forefinger together again and felt instantaneously calmer. He understood what was being implied and it was a tremendous shock to think that the man he had shared a home with and trusted with almost all of his affairs for so long could possibly be so treacherous and evil. He now felt embarrassed that he had been so furiously outraged that his confidents could think him so unaware of what happened under his very nose. He could now see intellectually that, as they had no other leads, Rupert had been involved previously in two deaths and had never gelled with Sara that he was worthy of their suspicion. Emotionally though, it still felt ridiculously and hideously unfeasible.

"Hugo," Jane said, hardly audibly "May I continue with this line of thought, even if just to eliminate it?"
He nodded unhappily and she continued very softly.
"I know from Jonathan that Rupert is rather eccentric, please can you tell me about that?"
She knew she sounded like a counsellor but that was probably no bad thing. She had started building up a professional client, therapist rapport with him this morning so she hoped her slightly authoritative approach would put him at his ease and gain the best from him. Jonathan looked on in awe. She was incredible and playing it just right. He hoped that one day he would be able to persuade her to lower the professional facade for him; the more he knew of her the more he wanted to know.

"Well...." began Hugo "I guess he's rather picky and pedantic but I find it amusing and sometimes even endearing. He's been a rock for me over the years and I'm finding it very hard to believe he would ever knowingly hurt me, even though I admit he didn't get on well with Sara."
"Do you know what the problem is there?"
"Not really. She always thought of him as a bit strange and unwelcoming. He doesn't really 'do' emotion and that threw Sara who is so open and loving."
"And how did he feel about her?"
"He was actually fairly dismissive of her. I think he's probably a misogynist to be honest. Sara always referred to him as the 'weirdo'!"

It had been easy to disregard Jane's misgivings about Rupert as she didn't know him but he supposed he had always ignored Sara's feelings about him too. He was really beginning to see the sense in Jane's concern and saw that he should take it seriously.
"I'm sorry," he finally apologised to his friends, "I can see that we have to look into this.

How do we go about it?" The practicalities of moving forward with the hypothesis left him totally at a loss and he felt more comfortable deferring to his cleverer companions.Jane and Jonathan felt both relieved and proud that he had been able to make this massive leap so quickly. Neither wanted to make a fuss but Jane leant over and squeezed Hugo's hand appreciatively.

"Try and eat something." She coaxed persuasively, gesturing toward his untouched plate and continued,

"How much do you know about his parents' deaths?"

"No more than I have told you really." He said picking at his chicken, "I was only thirteen at the time and overheard my mother and father discussing it after they had read about it in our local paper. We hadn't known that Mrs Jackson had been so poorly, bless her, she'd only been with us for a few weeks. Apparently she had suffered with depression for years and killed herself either purposefully or in confusion by taking too much of her prescribed medication. Her distraught husband, Rupert's father, walked out into the sea only days later leaving Rupert an orphan. The poor boy was sent to his aunt's house in Scotland where he stayed until he started at Bristol University and that's when I met up with him again. Surely we can't just go accusing him of..of..?" he trailed off, looking down and closing his eyes. Jane thought of passing him a tissue from her handbag but decided that, in public, he would prefer to just blink the tear away. Instead she said gently.

"Let's try and find out more about what happened and then we can talk about how best to tackle him."

"I'll see if Google can help" ever practical Jonathan said, reaching for his phone and his reading glasses. He searched and scrolled, occasionally mumbling as he read to himself until Hugo felt himself about to explode with impatience.

"Right." Jonathan said finally. "There are articles in the Dorset Echo about both deaths. Both were investigated by a Detective Blackthorpe. The pathologist found the cause of Helen's death as 'overdose' and Thomas's as 'drowning'. The coroner's recorded verdicts of 'accidental overdose' and 'suicide' and 'didn't believe there was anyone else involved' in either case. Detective Edward Blackthorpe's statement, read at the inquest into Mr Jackson's death, told how he had attended the death of Jackson's wife only five days before Jackson's suicide and that Jackson had found his wife dead on his return home from work. He also reported that this was one of the most tragic cases he had worked on." Jonathan removed his glasses so that he could see his associates' expressions.

Jane digested what she had heard then asked. "Is Rupert mentioned anywhere? Where was he when his mother passed away? Maybe I'm reading too much into it but I feel suspicious. Call it women's intuition if you like." What she didn't want to say in front of Hugo was that two deaths may not necessarily be suspicious but now that there was also Sara's disappearance, she had a very uncomfortable feeling.

"Please can you Google the detective Jonathan? We need to find out more." Obligingly, he once again donned his glasses and turned his attention to his phone.

Jacques cleared the table and left the bill, sensitively serving them without interruption. As soon as the waiter had left, Jonathan excitedly shared his new information.

"It seems that he retired six years ago unfortunately but I dug a little deeper and he's still living in Dorset. Furthermore, there's an article here about him being an active member of his amateur dramatics company." He paused with his own theatrical effect "And he's in Aladdin this week. He's playing the genie. They open tonight." He finished with a flurry.

Hugo and Jane were suitably impressed. The former swallowed hard. Was this really a step forward in being reunited with Sara? His friends were looking triumphant and he wondered, resentfully, if the excitement of their successful detective work was eclipsing the actual reason for it. He pressed his thumb and index finger together and focused on his breathing for a moment until he felt able to relax. Naturally, his friends couldn't be expected to feel as strongly about Sara as he did and, he reminded himself, they were doing him a very great favour. He looked up from his reverie when he realised that Jonathan was addressing him.

"Sorry, I was lost in my thoughts there for a minute." He said blushing.

97

"That's quite alright, old chap, don't worry at all, we know how hard this must be for you. I was just saying I think we should talk to Rupert and if we're not happy about his answers, go and see this Blackthorpe. We can tell the copper our fears, if he's good enough to listen and he should be able to confirm if there was anything at all suspicious about Helen and Thomas's deaths and whether that suspicion ever lay on Rupert." Jonathan spoke austerely. The three of them all took a moment to acknowledge the gravity of this proposition. Hugo broke the silence.

"My head's so mixed up! It keeps flitting and I don't know anymore whether I should be thinking of Rupert as my companion and employee, a thirteen year old orphan or an abductor."
Jane responded, sympathising with his difficulty.

"We could be talking about all three. We don't know yet but I think you need to stay open minded and I also think you need to stay strong. Meanwhile, we also have to accept that whilst this is our only explanation at the moment, there could well be another one that we know nothing of yet. Let's go and see Rupert now, and try to remove him as a suspect."
Uncomfortable with this idea, Hugo said "We can't just go in there mob handed and accuse the poor man of...of..." he paused, collecting his thoughts "I'll go, that'll look a lot more natural."

"Ok" Jane agreed "what will you say to him?"

"I'm not sure but am thinking clearly now, thank goodness, and will know when I'm there. I won't let him deflect me with his Rupertness."

She breathed deeply, knowing her next sentence would be particularly emotive. "Hugo, if Rupert can't help, I think you need to file a missing persons report."

"I can't!" he exclaimed, panic rising. "She said not to try and find her! I don't want to push her further away!" He was almost weeping.
Jane recognised the shock symptoms and saw that he was thinking historically, back to before he'd realised the letter wasn't genuine. She spoke quietly.

"It's been three days since she left and we now know that the note couldn't have been written freely by her. We need to get her back to you and that means doing everything we can to find her."

Hugo's mist cleared again. He hated how his thoughts kept getting so jumbled and felt stupid.

"Why didn't I realise earlier? What an idiot I am. How much unnecessary suffering have I caused her? I'll go and talk to Rupert now and depending on what he says, drive to Dorset tonight. Please will you come with me? And yes, you're right, the police must be told." Hugo felt better to have made these decisions.

"Of course we'll come with you and you're not an idiot at all, please don't be so hard on yourself." said Jonathan kindly, answering for both of them. "And I'll drive." He realised he may have been presumptuous and looked at Jane seeking reassurance.

"Then that's settled." Jane smiled "I think we should leave straight away, if Jonathan's ok driving back late tonight?" He nodded. "Then we won't need overnight bags. We'll wait outside you house for you and if we're going to Dorset you can phone the police from the car, if that's ok for you?" she asked Hugo "and I will call my neighbour to see to Ninja, she's really good with her. My cat." She added for Jonathan's benefit.

"Yes, that's fine" replied Hugo "and I feel happier how I know we're doing something positive. I'll just sort this bill out and we can go." he raised his hand at the protests. "It's the least I can do. I don't know how I'll ever repay you two for all your help and support. I'm really grateful, thank you."

Chapter Fifteen

Hugo had been out for the whole day, where the Dickens was he? He must have been quite drunk yesterday evening, judging by the meagre amount still left in the decanter but hadn't been too late or noisy when he'd returned and had left fairly early this morning. Both the drinking and staying out were quite out of character; it really was about time the man realised his pain in the neck of a girlfriend wasn't coming back, pulled himself together, and started to 'man up' as they called it now. Rupert was grossly disappointed in him and was saddened that he couldn't help but see parallels with his father who had also become weak and feeble after being freed from a millstone of a woman. Why couldn't these men see what was best for them? Curling his lip with contempt, he wondered why they allowed themselves to become so mesmerised, so bewitched? He was thankful that he was made of stronger stuff and would never let himself be swayed by the weaker sex.

Though he had never been able to depend on women, he had really looked up to his employer who had been the first man he'd trusted in a very long time and now he too was letting him down. Thinking of women, he pondered if he needed to be doing anything about the mess in the cellar yet. He would have to sort it out shortly but maybe he should wait another couple of days or so to avoid encountering any extra unpleasantness when he went down there. By which, he knew he meant, finding her alive. He wasn't entirely sure how long it would take but the task of clearing his impeccably tidy cellar was going to be nasty and difficult enough without further inconveniences and complications. He drew his dark eyebrows together in a frown as he realised his stupid oversight of not putting a large plastic sheet beneath her. It would have made things so much cleaner and easier as it would have served as both floor protector and makeshift bag. There would be all sorts of mess down there now, he grumbled to himself. His punishment for that mistake would be more work, he sighed. He would need to time the disagreeable deed fairly accurately because he'd have to catch her between rigor mortis and putrefaction. The idea was rather repellent to him, though probably only on a par with most people having to stuff a turkey, he acknowledged. Touching live human flesh was almost too much for him to stomach and this presumably would be worse but at least he wouldn't have to see those awful popping, beseeching eyes. He'd never had difficulty handling the animal carcasses from which he had learned about the death timeline but they had been encased with fur rather than the awful pale clammy dirty dermal material people were covered with. He preferred not to even touch his own skin but at least he knew it was as clean as it could be. As much as he'd always liked this house, it wasn't really the same without the Hugo he'd known and the task before him might taint it further; he wondered if maybe burning the thing down would be the easiest answer. He would have to give this some more thought.

Chapter Sixteen

2.15pm saw the three friends in Jonathan's four by four pulling up on Redcliffe Square. Hugo, feeling stronger than he had expected, let himself into his house and called out to Rupert. Whilst he didn't want to accept that the man he had known since childhood could be the perpetrator of such a heinous act he felt it was certainly time for firm questioning. He called out again.

"Rupert, I'd like a word with you. Now please" Rupert, from his rooms, heard an authoritative tone in Hugo's voice that he hadn't heard for a long time and decided it would be prudent not to respond. Receiving no reply, Hugo strode over to Rupert's door and delivered a sharp rat-a-tat and a further

"Rupert!"

The PA hardly ever left the house, he had no outside interests or friends so this absence was a mystery. Could Jane's suspicions have been totally off the mark and in fact another of his closest circle been abducted? This was terrible.

"Rupert" he shrilled and to the apparently empty house

"Right, that's it, I'm phoning the police!"

Rupert who needed their interference even less than a conversation with his erstwhile master, emerged from his quarters with no explanation for his tardiness.

"Thank God you're alright." Hugo was visibly relieved. "I thought you had been taken too." Rupert looked at him incredulously as he realised the proposed call to the constabulary had been for his safety and not his questioning.

"No, as you see, I am here and I am safe." He adopted his smile mask.

Recovering from his fears of a double abduction, Hugo remembered why he had come and his loss and anger bit into him harder than ever exacerbated by Rupert's calmness. The absence of emotion which had once relaxed him suddenly made his blood boil. How dare he stand there smiling so smugly?

"Rupert, is there anything about Sara's disappearance that you haven't told me? Anything at all?"

"Of course not. What could there be?"

To Hugo, it sounded like a challenge, a throwing down of a gauntlet. Superciliousness didn't constitute guilt but it certainly made him angry.

"I know you've had a shock but wouldn't it be easier for you if you moved on now?"

Hugo couldn't believe what he was hearing; it may as well have been 'there are plenty more fish in the sea'!

"If there's nothing else?" Rupert raised his eyebrows enquiringly for an instant before slithering back to his rooms. Hugo's blood seemed to drop a hundred degrees and a shiver ran down his spine.

Minutes later he was describing what had happened to Jane and Jonathan as they tackled London's traffic, thanking their lucky stars they were able to avoid the city centre. For the first time, the true gravity of the situation touched them all; they also realised that what they were now embarking on was precarious to say the least; they were expecting this poor retired copper to be interested in answering their questions. The man must have gone through weeks of rehearsals, would no doubt be very relieved to have put on his first performance and be looking forward to a celebratory drink with his co stars before taking an early night to prepare for the following day's show. They would have called ahead to make an appointment had there been any time and had they known how to contact him but those luxuries had been absent. They appreciated that they were catching him very much on the hop and would have to be very ingratiating indeed and also ensure that he didn't feel press ganged. They decided that it should therefore be Jane who should approach him and do the talking, she was the most gentle of them and being very pretty wouldn't do any harm. She wasn't desperate to be the one to interrogate the gentleman but admitted she was probably the most concise and the least emotional for the job. They also thought it would be best if Jonathan sat in the car whilst they talked to him and he was more than happy with that. By the time they joined the M25 they had a much clearer idea of the details.

From his position in the back, Hugo could observe Jane and Jonathan in the passenger and driver's seats. He had the bizarre feeling of being a child again in his parent's car, still cocooned in the safety and stability he'd always assumed was his birthright. If only his little daydream could be true and the events of the last few days had not yet happened, were far off in the future where they could be avoided, circumvented. The two of them looked every inch the couple. Many men would have bitterly resented their closeness when their own relationship had taken such an enormous blow but kindly Hugo felt only pleasure that he could have facilitated this union for his friend, he just wished to God that it could have been in any other circumstances. He was happy he had the back seat to himself as it afforded him time to think; he had been on such a roller coaster of emotion since Friday. There had been times he had felt that there had been some sort of crazy misunderstanding and Sara would just reappear in a haze of cashmere and diaphanous hair and at others that this was the start of an unimaginably horrifying nightmare in which he spent his whole life missing and searching for the only woman he could ever love. Today had given him more of a glimmer of hope than he'd felt thus far. The hypnotherapy had not only slain the dragon of his distrust of it but provided much needed clarity and calm. He felt positive about doing something constructive toward finding Sara and the next thing he had to do was make the call to the police. As much as he knew it was the correct thing to do and practically could only help, he was dreading making Sara's disappearance even more concrete by officially filing a report.

He pressed his thumb and forefinger together hard for a few seconds, took his iPhone from his camel coat pocket and before he could procrastinate further, took a deep breath and dialled 101.

"Hello, Thames Valley Police, which force do you require?" asked a recorded voice. After asking for "Metropolitan, er, Kensington and Chelsea" he was put on hold and was informed several times by the disembodied voice that his call was very important to it and he would be answered shortly. Eventually after being sorely tempted more than once, despite his better judgement, to hang up, he was put through to the control room of his local station.

He explained as succinctly as possible about Sara's disappearance, with occasional interrupting input from the front of the car. The officer listened silently, asking questions and seeking clarification where necessary until he had all the information that he needed for the missing persons report. The policeman then explained that another officer would call round in the next few days to take more details and any photographs Hugo had of Sara. Hugo was just about to question the 'next few days' when the voice on the other end of the line told him that it wouldn't be considered an emergency as all her relatives and friends had already been told, she was an adult and had left an explanatory note.

Hugo tried in vain to argue, to reiterate what he thought he had already made clear but the PC clearly thought he was just another jilted lover in denial. Hugo could feel his pity, almost hear him thinking what a poor sap he was being dumped just ten days before Christmas. Hugo understood that they were no doubt struggling on a skeleton staff at this time of year and were overstretched with revellers, drunks and prank calls but his ability to empathise didn't, for a second, alleviate his frustration at not being given credence to. He made and failed at several attempts to penetrate the thwarting wall of narrow mindedness that had been built up before him.

Crushed, he continued to stare vacantly at the phone screen long after it had gone blank. Jane and Jonathan had heard enough from his side of the conversation to understand fully what had been said and felt his pain, disappointment and frustration. They made the unspoken decision to sit silently and give him time to come to terms with the harsh and unfair decision, acknowledging that he knew they were there for him whenever he felt ready.

....

Sara shook herself slightly in an effort to try and clear the fog that clouded her head but the searing bolt of pain it caused stilled her at once. She was utterly disorientated, seeming to ricochet between being confused by the changing images presenting themselves before her and totally buying into the validity of whichever scene of the

105

sometimes grotesque, sometimes comforting, always surreal imagery that played out on the movie screen of her mind. She tried to grasp any semblance of reality to make sense of the slippery fish of her lapsing sanity. She wondered where her grandparents were, it had been nice to have seen them again but more than anything else she badly wanted Hugo to come back. He and the gigantic cuddly toy had swirled away with one of her old school friends and Professor Thompson and they'd all been singing...conscious...half conscious... partially remembered visions blurring into one in a swirling ...sometimes pulsating mass of colour and light. Half sleep...half light...half life... Caught between dream and reality...trapped in a limbo where time and space were irrelevant and meaningless. Good and evil co-joining in a meeting of fantasy and fear...beauty morphing into the grotesque...angel's and devil's faces dancing before hers...

Sara drifted periodically and temporarily to wakefulness...to somewhere approaching awareness . She wished she knew what day it was...whether it was day...or night...how long she had struggled to free herself from this nightmare of imperfect illusion and distorted actuality...but then it didn't seem important and she slid back into dream state. From time to time she had thought she was aware of people round her...her late grandparents of course...and old school friends she hadn't seen for years... Were these spirit people and was it her time to be escorted and helped away from this confusion? The concept of that felt comforting rather than frightening. Sometimes she thought she was being prepared...purified to make that final journey....sometimes she just felt a nothingness... She seemed to travel between a dark, cold netherworld and the strange and not quite familiarity of her own home... She was too weak to call out and her throat was too sore anyway...and she was too sleepy...Sometimes she felt herself floating away from...from...where was she? This wasn't her bed... It was cold and dark and she was bewildered and frightened...why couldn't she think straight? She floated without aim... wondering vaguely what might be the implications of not returning...but only really in a formless...musing...interested sort of way. She was sooo cold...so much in pain...so blind...so immersed in another world she wasn't familiar with... where nothing and no one mattered...

....

Hugo closed his eyes and imagined a time when this was all over and he and Sara were cuddled up on the sofa in front of the fire. He visualised them sharing the fleecy throw, Eskimo kissing and planning their wedding. For maybe a couple of seconds he felt an intense and all encompassing joy before the current truth shattered his paradise, slaughtering his happiness. He gulped back stinging tears and to keep himself sane, made a deal with himself. He could enjoy this daydream for a full five minutes longer as long as he then turned his attention fully to seriously making plans for the constructive process of this evening's meeting.

He took himself back to the Chesterfield, to the roaring fire, to the smell of Sara's flawless skin and hair as he nuzzled his face into her golden mane. He wrapped his arms more tightly around her beautiful and fragile body and she snuggled against him, brushing her lips lightly against his, whispering how very much she loved him.

....

There he was! How she had missed him, she disliked to be parted even just for the length of a phone call. She opened her arms to him and he leaned forward kissing her gently before swinging himself onto the sofa and arranging the fleece over both of them. She was sooo lucky to have him....he was completely perfect. She ruffled his gorgeous hair and hugged him tightly.

....

He had never loved anybody like this. The few failed relationships he had experienced in the past paled dully into insignificance, were as nothing compared to the strength of the feelings he felt for his dear angel.

....

She looked into his eyes and felt as though her heart would burst, that it was not strong enough to hold all the love she felt for him. He was the most truly beautiful thing that had ever happened to her.

....

He cupped her delicate little chin in his hand and kissed the tip of the very prettiest of pretty noses.

....

She looked into his eyes and saw through them into his faultless and beautiful soul, knowing that she would always be with him.

....

He knew this wasn't the conventional way to do it but he couldn't help himself.
"I want to marry you...please marry me...please be my wife."

....

She saw the look in his eyes...she'd known before he had started to talk what he was going to say. "Yes, darling, yes, of course, it would make me the happiest girl in the world."

....

This was the most amazing moment of his life. He had thought she would accept but to hear her words was the most beautiful sound he had ever heard.

....

She couldn't wait to move into this lovely house with him...to be married to him, to know he was hers always. Her grandparents were back. How lovely, she couldn't wait to tell someone their exciting news.

. . . .

He had never ever been happier; he was filled with a warm glow of adoration.

. . . .

The sliver of light gleaming through the slightly ajar door glowed larger...her grandmother held her hand out to her..

"Come, we'll look after you now..." Sara was confused but Hugo would explain....where was he though..? Had he had another phone call...? Why couldn't she remember..?

"Don't worry sweetheart, follow me... your grandfather's waiting to see you too." Her grandmother's voice comforted her as it always had. She squinted against the light and was glad her head wasn't hurting anymore...that nothing was hurting anymore... She allowed her grandmother to lead her to the door. Her grandfather took her other hand. The walk up the steps to the open door was effortless; they seemed to float gracefully... She felt peaceful and safe as they both gently squeezed her hands and smiled sweetly at her...

Chapter Seventeen

Hugo had loved his wonderful fantasy, hadn't wanted to leave it but knew he had been self indulgent enough so dragged himself unhappily back to reality and resolved to set his mind to their forthcoming conversation with Blackthorpe and how they were going to coax him into helping them. He could see why Jonathan was so infatuated with Jane, she really was a marvel as he said; if anyone could persuade a tired, stressed actor to discuss a decade old case with complete strangers, it was she. He didn't feel he was over exaggerating when he felt that his whole future was hanging on this communication and even though he had known the hypnotherapist for only a short time, he couldn't think of anyone he'd rather trust. He believed that with her natural womanly wiles and her mesmerizing voice, she would be able to gently cajole the detective into disclosing to them that he had indeed felt a niggling but undefined discomfort about the male youth and, now, in the light of their new suspicions, would want to help. Hugo imagined the ex policeman being so impressed by their detective skills that he would be prepared to guide them through the next stage of the process which, though abhorrent at first, was now welcome. If Rupert had been a traitor and murderer all this time, heartlessly making a fool and a victim out of his friend and employer he deserved everything and more that the law could throw at him.

....

The M25 was unfortunately doing a rather good impression of a car park and the daylight was already beginning to fade. The nights would begin to draw out in just six days, the winter's back would be broken and light would, once again, replace darkness. Exhausted Hugo's eyes were closed, Jane observed and hoped he was sleeping, he desperately needed it. He would require all his wits over the coming days and sleep deprivation would hinder him deeply. She was glad she had been able to offer him some resources as she felt he could well be about to be pushed to further limits, depending on the outcome of her dialogue with Blackmore. She was optimistic about the impending conversation but was intelligent enough to know it would need careful handling. She was, if totally honest, not as hopeful about poor Sara's fate and feared that time was very much of the essence. Whoever had taken Sara, Rupert, as they suspected, or someone else, hadn't made any demands and it seemed unlikely they would go to the trouble of keeping her indefinitely. It seemed far more likely, she admitted reluctantly to herself, that they didn't intend to keep her and more likely still, hadn't kept her. The euphemism made the idea slightly more palatable to her but she undoubtedly couldn't voice her worries to Hugo, the poor man must have enough demons of his own to keep at bay. If she could manoeuvre a situation where she could be alone with Jonathan, she would like to share her fears with him.

With just this mere thought, she was surprised at her body's reaction. She knew that there were circumstances where clients became friends, became more than friends but she personally had no experience of them and had, in her ignorance, always disapproved strongly of such things. This, she scolded herself, was no way to be using up her limited time; she should be planning how she could best win over Detective Blackmore. He must have masses of experience in finding missing people so his help would be invaluable to them. Their plan was to all watch the pantomime and she would go and wait at the stage door after the performance. Hopefully the Aladdin's genie wouldn't take too long to get changed and remove his stage make-up; she didn't fancy standing in the sub zero December weather for too long. She thought she would begin by ingratiating herself through praising the company's and particularly his performance and then ask if he would be kind enough to give her a few minutes of his precious and limited time. She would then, hopefully back indoors, give him a succinct description of what had happened followed by an explanation of why they had chosen him. She hoped her brevity and consideration would help hold his attention and make him more inclined to listen. She was quite confident that he would be forthcoming; it would be rather churlish of him not to be and pretty unlikely in a professional used to helping people, even though he was retired.

....

Jonathan drove in silence. He could see that both Hugo and Jane had their eyes closed and if not asleep, were choosing to retreat into the privacy of their own thoughts. The flow of traffic was frustratingly slow but at least it allowed him to steel rare, unobserved glimpses of Jane; he watched her beautiful face and graceful hands folded neatly in her lap. As his heart reached out to her, he had an almost irrepressible urge to place his hand comfortingly onto her arm. Even in such anxious circumstances, it had been wonderful spending so much time with her but he knew that it was only because of the current state of affairs that they had been drawn so closely together and that soon it would come to an end. He was keenly aware that he was setting himself up for a fall but still, he intended to cherish every moment because the more he knew of her, the more respect he amassed. She had been amazing with Hugo; she had held him together when he had been sure to shatter apart. He didn't think they would have got him, sanely, this far without her serenity, patience and understanding. He was certain that Blackmore would react well to her and with the copper's help, they would bring Sara safely home. As the road started to clear a little, he glanced again at her beautiful and peaceful profile and wondered if she were as calm inside as she seemed; whilst he was sure she could handle tonight, they all knew what was hanging on it.

....

Jonathan swung the Discovery into a car park bay and pulled on the handbrake. He was always relieved to reach a destination; he was happy to drive but had never felt he was a natural behind the wheel and didn't seem to find it as relaxing and rewarding as a lot of people did. He and Jane had been talking since they'd peeled off the motorway but only minimally; it had seemed disrespectful to make chit chat when Hugo was suffering so badly, the same reason he hadn't put the radio on. They had made good time on the A roads

112

and still had over an hour until the curtains went up so decided to go into the pub that stood between them and the little theatre. After a quick freshen up, they all shunned meals in favour of sandwiches; it had been a long day already and even though none of them had finished their lunches, they found that they had little appetite.

． ． ． ． ． ． ． ． ． ．

The three reluctant panto goers managed the absolute minimum 'oh yes he dids' and 'he's behind yous' as they could politely get away with. They were the only adults in the audience that were unaccompanied by children; Jane vaguely wondered how that looked. She tried, with little success, to picture the ridiculous, over weight man in green chiffon and gold turban, investigating the double death of Rupert's parents. She wanted to get this out of the way now, over and done with. At last the show was finally finished and the applause ended. Jonathan wished them luck and she and Hugo made their way to the back door that they had located before buying their tickets and finding their seats.

． ． ． ． ． ． ． ． ． ．

Jonathan was nervous in his powerlessness and hadn't taken his eyes off the car park entrance for the six and a half minutes he'd been waiting. There they were now; he swallowed hard as he made out in the darkness that their heads were bowed as the pair hurried along the rows parked cars and hoped that they were just protecting themselves from the piercing cold. Jane manoeuvred herself into the front passenger seat as Hugo slid into the back and they snapped in their seats belt without speaking to him or each other.

Jane had taken the responsibility of being the negotiator as she treated her whole life, with seriousness and gravity. She wasn't used to failing; was adept at not partaking in activities where success wasn't likely but tonight she had failed in her belief that she could sweet talk Blackthorpe thus bringing about the collapse of their mission. She had had to do this, she had shared her new friends' belief that she had been their best shot but she had let Hugo down.

When at last she started speaking, her words spilled from her like a mindstream, uncensored, telling of her anger and disappointment in herself and her embarrassment at being turned away almost immediately by the ex copper who believed them to be cranks. Not taking 'no' for an answer she had followed him, continuing doggedly to illicit his support, practically begging for aid which was not forthcoming and merely causing herself further humiliation; God, he had even actually referred to them as an crazy amateur sleuths and advised them to listen to the professionals whom she had explained had more or less said to just accept Sara had left Hugo. Her final attempt for help as he climbed into his cab had been to press him about the Jackson cases. He had barked that, no, he had not suspected the son or he would have investigated him and was she suggesting he had not done his job properly? She had apologised profusely and pushed Hugo's business card and a recent photograph of Sara into his leather gloved hand. She stopped her narration and breathed; it could not have gone more badly and she was mortified. Hugo had been stunned by the unequivocal rebuff and stood, ineffectively, watching Jane doing everything she could to help him. Despite feeling intense disappointment and disbelief at what had just happened, he muttered an acknowledgement that she could have done no more and his grateful thanks.

. . . .

The journey was slow and cheerless; each of them hiding in their own contemplations, processing their feelings alone. A haze of shock, resentment, dismay, loss of hope, incredulity, horror and guilt hung in unequal parts over the car's occupants. It was Jane that broke the hush.

"I'm sorry I messed up," she started huskily after the prolonged period of quiet, "I know it's late and we're all tired and disappointed but Hugo really shouldn't go home alone so we need to work out our next move. Let's stop at the next service station and get a drink, yes?"

114

The men had already told her she had nothing to be sorry for, that she had done her best but they told her again and agreed that a coffee, a rest and discussing a new plan was a good idea. Fifteen minutes later, the Land Rover pulled off the M3 and into Fleet services.

The Starbucks was mercifully still open and they ordered coffees and muffins from the barista who seemed glad of something to do. She served them cake, drink and eager chit chat, the latter of which was disappointingly, for her, mainly ignored. The place was understandably deserted at this late or rather early hour so, at a distance from the coffee shop, they were able to talk unheard. After ten minutes of upsettingly unproductive dialogue their solitude was interrupted by the outside door being hurriedly tugged open, allowing in way too much cold air...and Sara.

Jane, who had her back to the entrance shivered violently, pulled her coat tighter around her chilled body, muttered quietly to herself and then halted mid grumble as she heard Jonathan's sharp intake of breath and saw the colour draining out of Hugo's face. They both looked as though they had seen an apparition; jaws hanging open slackly and motionless. Suddenly and without warning, Hugo sprang into action from his stillness as if electrified, leapt from his seat and practically flew across the room with Jonathan immediately behind him. This was her, this time there was no mistake; this was her beautiful and slender body, her posture, her gait, her hair, her skin. He skidded to a halt just inches away from her, gasping her name.
"Sara, oh Sara, I can't believe it! Thank God"
She looked at him, taken aback; their eyes locked as they shared a frozen moment. In a strong Midlands accent, answered.
"Sorry bab, I think you've got the wrong person. I'm Roxy, very pleased to meet you." She extended Sara's hand.

Hugo deflated, the power, once again having deserted him; he didn't understand what was happening. Was he dreaming, was this a nightmare? What the hell was going on? He put his hand out to a table to steady himself as his world shifted. He could see Sara's lips moving but instead of her dulcet tones, this outlandish voice was coming out of his Sara's mouth. His head swam and his knees started to buckle beneath him; as if in slow motion Jonathan and Jane linked their arms through his, supporting his limp frame and manoeuvring him into a chair. Regaining his self-possession, Hugo joined by his friends gawped at the poor lookalike who would have been decidedly intimidated had she been made of less strong stuff. Instead she laughed.

"You'll look like you've seen a ghost! Either that or I didn't notice something terribly odd with my hair last time I looked in the mirror!"

Jonathan spoke first. "We're sorry, we really are" he stammered "but you're the absolute double of our friend, the absolute double! She went missing last week and we thought you were her."
Now as Hugo looked more closely, this girl's hair was a little dry at the ends and her eyes were maybe not quite as grey as his Sara's, yet she could be her identical twin.

"I've never been anyone's spitting image before" the girl chuckled "maybe it was fate you met me?" She was dressed in torn jeans, as was the fashion and a loose red sweatshirt. By her side was an old, fully packed rucksack which she had dropped when Hugo had first run over, not knowing whether she should be preparing to defend herself. At first glance, one would have thought that she was dressed in the uniform of most students but on closer inspection, she was a little dirtier, a little more dishevelled. Jonathan glanced at Jane's pretty but sensible flat leather shoes, smart knee length woollen skirt and neat turtle necked sweater. She probably looked a few years older than her twenty-five, but perfectly professional and elegant. Looking back at the waif he wondered if the rucksack contained her travelling things or her entire life. He said;

"Please join us, may we buy you a coffee and something to apologise for scaring you?"

"Yeah that'd be cool thanks. I'm kind of at a loose end. Long story" she beamed.

She had had a rough time recently. Her parents and she had been estranged for several years on account of her falling pregnant five years ago when she was fifteen. They had initially tried to make the

116

best of it but she had miscarried the baby at six months which had been a terrible loss to her; only deepened by her parents' poorly hidden celebrations. She had left them and their home in the rather nice Birmingham suburb in which she had grown up and gone to live with a group of friends, including the baby's father in a shared house in a much rougher part of town. The semi that they rented from the landlord, whilst he decided what to do with it, had been little more than a squat so they'd got it for a minimal rent and acted more or less as caretakers keeping it safe from actual squatters. Roxanne had existed rather than lived there but had thrown herself effectively into the unfamiliar lifestyle, learning quickly from the other tenants who were more used to the set up. Her parents had visited once; they felt it was time to get over their dashed dreams for the sake of a relationship with the daughter who had once had her life at her feet. They had baulked at the squalor and the damp but the cockroaches that Roxanne referred to as 'the pets' had been too much for the middle aged, middle class couple and they fled declaring that neither forgiving nor forgetting were possible. They had let their anger, their judgment and their ego overcome the erstwhile love they had held for Roxanne; whilst it's said that love wins out, it hadn't in this case and whilst Roxanne acknowledged it as a terrible waste, she wasn't prepared to lower herself further by begging for their attention, their money or their time.

A month ago when she and indeed the rest of the country had been happily getting ready for Christmas, she had discovered her young man, who admittedly had never been the best of boyfriends, in bed with one of the other tenants. She left immediately and had been uncomfortably and reluctantly living on peoples' sofas and goodwill ever since. None of her former 'friends' had attempted to find her and she knew she had to start rebuilding her life in the New Year once employers were recruiting again. She had always worked in cafes or shops whilst her housemates had been happy to rely on benefits and she wasn't prepared to live on charity now.

Jonathan escorted Roxanne off to the counter whilst the others made their way back to their table. When they returned several minutes later with an enormous grande cup of hot chocolate piled high with cream and marshmallows and two muffins 'because she hadn't been able to choose between chocolate and blueberry' neither of the waiting friends had said a word; Hugo because he was still too stunned by all the evenings events and Jane because she was deep in thought. Once they were all settled, Jonathan formally introduced everybody and, though not entirely certain why, decided to tell their new friend the whole sorry saga.

"Well," Roxanne whistled when he had finished, "that's some story. Do you really think this Rupert could be so evil? The police obviously don't but then I no longer trust them as far as I can throw them." She snorted then remembering her manners added. "This must be really, really horrible for you Hugo, I'm sorry. Wish I could help."

This gorgeous looking red head was certainly hurting and her heart as a fellow deserted soul went out to him but she didn't buy the abduction tale for one second and wasn't over impressed with his friends' over indulgence either. People left people all the time for all sorts of reasons and you just had to get over it. This farce was just prolonging his agony; let the guy off with his dignity relatively intact rather than shooting off like a mixture of a Charlie's Angels style vigilante group and an Enid Blyton-esque 'Three go mad in Dorset'. Jane, who had been sitting in her characteristic thinking 'steepled fingers beneath chin' pose, spoke before Hugo had to, directing her words to Roxanne.

"Were you serious when you offered to help?"

Roxanne thought she may as well join in with the charade for now as she wasn't exactly awash with alternatives and nodded enthusiastically, sending as cascade of Triple Belgian Chocolate Muffin across the table.

"Sure, why not? I need something to take my mind off stuff."

"If Hugo and Jonathan still have faith in me and agree," Jane stated rather nervously "then I wonder if you wouldn't mind accompanying Hugo to his house, and pretending to be Sara? If Rupert is involved, his reaction to you should give him away and then hopefully we'll know for sure and be able to extract from him where he's taken her. What do you all think?" She was aware the idea sounded preposterous but also that it was crazy enough to actually work.

Jonathan agreed immediately that he thought it an excellent idea. Hugo was still stunned; it was completely surreal sitting with this Sara who wasn't Sara in the early hours of the morning surrounded by Christmas paraphernalia in an empty service station after the day he's endured. He didn't think he could take much more. Roxanne decided she was more than happy to play along if they were going to carry on feeding her like this. She didn't agree with their beliefs, methods or strategy but they were well meaning and generous and she needed the break right now, especially if it meant spending time with a cute guy. She definitely intended to turn her attention to sorting out her life and maybe rejoining the education system very shortly but meanwhile these people were obviously at least comfortably well off and if she could be useful in return for their kindness it seemed like a win-win situation.

'The four musketeers' as Roxanne had privately dubbed herself and her new compatriots, discussed the practicalities. Jonathan would drop her and Hugo off and her temporary host would sneak her in past Rupert who he felt confidently certain would be asleep and oblivious of their entry. He had a spare bed she could sleep in and some of Sara's clothes for her to wear tomorrow. It seemed monstrous to Hugo that he should be dressing another woman in his girlfriend's outfits but this girl was acting very kindly and whilst his reasoning faculties appeared to have closed down, he trusted Jane that it was a good idea.

Roxanne could feel her excitement rising; not in a million years could she have envisioned her day turning out like this. Her last lift of the day had dropped her off at the services because it was the nearest to his destination, London. She'd been trying really unsuccessfully to hitchhike there for three days; people didn't feel safe giving you a ride anymore. The Smoke, with its streets all paved with gold seemed the place to go but she hadn't wanted to arrive there late at night. It was the right place to go to seek your fame and fortune, right? She had expected to snooze here like she had at Oxford Services on the M40 the previous night and grab a wash in the morning before the commuters and holiday makers started invading what, during the night, were her private bathroom facilities. When she had embarked on what had perhaps been a foolhardy expedition to the capital, she'd known her options were running out and it had been in a 'what's the worst that can happen?' gung-ho frame of mind. Whilst there had been times she'd feared she'd never feel properly warm, clean or comfortable again, it now seemed to be working out not too badly after all.

Chapter Eighteen

Edward Blackthorpe didn't feel like going to bed. He was unsettled, troubled and feeling very guilty about having sent that woman and her friend away so abruptly; they had caught him on the back foot but he knew that was no excuse for such ungentlemanly behaviour. He should not have given the duo such short shrift; the poor woman hadn't deserved the flea that he had left in her ear. Still having had stage make up behind his own ears with a splitting head ache and harbouring a disappointment with their first performance his detective hat couldn't have felt further away. There had been a general level of apathy amongst many of the cast members tonight which he was unaccustomed to in the world of amateur dramatics. The word 'amateur' had never sat well with him. In its true sense, of course, it was correct but in his experience, many amateur actors though not as skilled or proficient, treated their roles almost as 'professionally' as the professionals. However, tonight's weak and lacklustre production had felt wishy washy; despite his feelings of anti-climax, he amused himself with the pun. The humour lifted his spirits sufficiently to make him realise that his self indulgence of wallowing in disappointment was merely serving to avoid the even less comfortable shame about his reprehensible manners; which he had to rectify.

He reflected on the double case the pair had been interested in. It had been rather grim when the news hit his team that the newly bereaved husband had chosen to walk out into the cold British sea and been sucked away by its cruel currents. Both deaths had been tragically unfortunate; the damaged wife had been an accident waiting to happen for years and after finding her, Thomas Jackson, racked with a barrage of feelings from horror to guilt hadn't been able to live with himself. Their barely adolescent son had been questioned by both one of his officers and by Ed himself; he had undoubtedly been strange. Blackmore recalled that the boy hadn't once cried; it had been assumed he was on the spectrum somewhere but he had never been diagnosed or seriously suspected of either death. It was an interesting coincidence though that the adult Rupert was now mixed up in, if this woman were to believed, a suspicious disappearance. Blackthorpe had been a policeman long enough to know that when the word 'coincidence' cropped up, it shouldn't be ignored.

He had been retired for some time so could not do anything official but after being so ill-mannered he felt he should, at least, give them some advice about how best to get the local force involved. He fished in his pocket and pulled out the card and photograph the woman had given him. The card was the man's evidently and displayed his address; the photo was of the 'missing' girl who appeared very distinctive with her pale elfin face and what he thought might be called ash blonde hair. He decided spontaneously that he would take a trip to see them tomorrow but that he wouldn't call them in advance as it wasn't fair to raise their hopes when he didn't know how much he could realistically help. London at this time of year would be very festive and his wife would be thrilled to go shopping at the gigantean Shepherds Bush Westfields. She deserved a bit of fun and he knew she'd love being able to choose Christmas gifts in the town of a place for their two sons; she'd been saying for weeks that she had exhausted their local shopping centre and time was running out to buy presents; she didn't like having to give money.

Having resolved to check out their story the following day his conscious felt clear enough to put today's events behind him, have a small whisky, give the good news to his better half and get an early night in preparation for his 8am start, two long drives, investigations and evening performance; this would be his penance for being rude, he thought wryly but thinking about it, a bit of detective work could actually be fun after so long.

Chapter Nineteen

Jane lay in bed, wide awake, eyes open, nauseous with fatigue, trying to quieten her restless mind. It was analysing and over analysing the day's events, racing through conversations and experiences, retracing its steps, cart wheeling, somersaulting, chastising, lamenting, congratulating, cringing; she felt like she were on some sort of fairground ride and didn't like it one bit. She was angry with herself for failing to stop her mind hurtling around when she knew she needed to rest; it had been a long day and if anyone knew how to relax it should have been her; physician heal thyself! Yet she was failing, for the second time in one day. She heaved her tired body out of bed, dislodging a confused and dishevelled Ninja and dragged her hooded fleece dressing gown from the back of her white wicker chair swathing herself in its cosy swathes. Shivering, she made her way down to the kitchen almost tripping over the cat that was now slaloming through the legs of the less agile biped who was already cursing herself for attempting to negotiate the stairs in the semi darkness. She'd read somewhere that eighty-six thousand people a year in the UK went to hospital because they'd fallen over their pets. Apparently dogs were seven times more likely to cause these accidents but that still left a lot of guilty cats and Jane didn't want to add to the two hundred daily average. Black cats on dark nights were practically invisible and tiny, quick Ninja circled her owner's ankles excitedly and recklessly without even using the sense she was born with. Having successfully reaching the ground floor without mishap and in one piece, Jane reached down lovingly and stroked the midnight velvet head. People said that cats were intelligent and had a way of looking directly into your soul but Jane was fairly sure that, although Ninj looked a little like omniscient Yoda, she was almost certainly merely wondering when the fridge door would next be opening.

Jane gingerly switched on the kitchen light hoping this would reduce the retina tormenting glare; it didn't. She filled the kettle to the maximum line and put it on the stove; she sometimes thought she should get an electric kettle but the design and nostalgic feel of her old fashioned one outweighed its disadvantages. She hunted for the Horlicks whilst it boiled and triumphant at finding it, decided she may as well open the shortbread biscuits as well. To stop the furry one begging, Jane gave her a piece of ham, not that this tactic had ever worked before. The whistle bit into the silence informing her it was time to drink and eat. She made the malted drink and a hot water bottle which she carried along with her 'several hours after midnight' feast into the sitting room and curled up in her easy chair with her legs tucked beneath her. Ninja sprang up and padded her lap through the fluffy dressing gown, filling the silence of the night with her purring. Jane kissed her noisy little companion on the top of her downy head, dipped a biscuit into her comforting milky drink and tried to untangle her thoughts. She had purposely left the lamp off and the diffused light from the kitchen was casting soft and soothing shadows against the walls. She sipped her Horlicks and sighed; she couldn't help still being disappointed with herself for letting down poor Hugo by allowing her task with Blackthorpe to defeat her. Now they had another solution in the form of the scruffy but sweet Sara double she really should be able to let it go but it still rankled that she'd lost her touch. That was ageing for you, she thought sardonically.

Jane took another sip of her comforting hot drink, stroked the now sleeping ball of fur and concentrated on her breathing as she had taught many of her clients. She felt the physical tension start to fade but as soon as she began to gently ease away the embarrassment of her failure, unbidden, disquieting and frankly unwelcome thoughts about Jonathan rushed in to take their place. What was wrong with her? He was her client for God's sake and she was a professional; or at least she'd always thought she was. She realised now, that it had been easy being ethical when there was no temptation and now an attraction had been introduced, she had managed to fall at the very first hurdle. She felt like a stupid teenager, not being able to think straight around this man; it had taken all her strength of control not to take his hand when it had been resting on his thigh while he drove. She was certain this feeling was mutual which fuelled it further; he was rubbish at hiding his attraction, bless him. How ridiculous; she was supposed to be quieting her mind s she could sleep. These feelings were not only distracting but inappropriate; if she were going to fall for every Tom, Dick or Harry that came into her consulting rooms her business would soon be in tatters! Yet she knew she was being hard on herself; this wasn't just one of a string of magnetisms, it felt real, it felt serious. She wasn't used to letting down her guard or trusting people very easily; it had been a long time since she'd even looked at a man so she knew this was special. She gave up on the idea of sleep for the time being and surrendered herself to her thoughts.

She had moved to London some four years earlier with her childhood sweetheart, Justin, when he'd managed to land a very well paid marketing job in the city straight after university and had been happy to support them both. She'd devotedly followed him, ignoring her own degree and leaving her separated parents whom she adored and her entire social network behind. It had been an unprecedented act of spontaneity. She had never been a rebellious, frivolous or even playful young person; having been brought up an only child of two lecturers versed in child psychology she had generally preferred to be in the company of their adult students rather than people of her own age. She had been valued and respected and had grown up quickly. Her parents had parted, as amicably as is possible, when Jane was eleven and she had lived in both of their houses which were less than one mile apart, on a weekly rotation. She'd had a bedroom with a desk, toys and a wardrobe of clothes in each home and had extremely fond memories of her childhood.

She had remained close to both her mother and father, spoke on the phone to each of them every week and visited her home town of Leamington Spa at least three times a year. She knew that they had been disappointed when she had sacrificed her career for her boyfriend's when they'd raised her to be independent but had respected her decision and seemed to be genuinely proud of her now. She had only lasted as a 'housewife' in those early London days for a few weeks and had soon booked herself on a two year counselling and hypnotherapy course.

She'd been the youngest of the fifteen candidates but had been mature and open thinking enough to learn to understand herself and others in a way that had frightened three people off the course. She'd been able to appreciate that it wasn't possible to comprehend and empathise with others' troubles until you could comprehend your own and had passed with flying colours. Over the last two years she had built a practice that now gave her a full time salary.

Unfortunately, whilst she had been getting to know herself, Justin had been getting to know one of his female colleagues and with his usual imperfect timing, just before Jane's final exams, he had moved out to live with her. Jane had been deeply wounded but had become expertly skilled at supporting herself emotionally as well as financially; she hadn't planned on changing her strategy. Yet, because of this man Jonathan, all of a sudden she was seeing everything differently and not only reconnecting with her deeply hidden feminine and vulnerable side but also noticing the beauty and magic around her. She found herself actually looking forward to Christmas for the first time in three years. The idea of Christmas made her think of mistletoe and she giggled quietly. Alone in her dimly lit room she felt herself blush; damn, she'd really let him get under her skin and she was fast becoming smitten.

Chapter Twenty

Jonathan's alarm went off at 6.45am. He glared at it through bleary eyes as if it were the personification of all evil and hit the snooze button. Four hours sleep was not e-bloody-nough at his age! Again the confounded thing sounded; surely it hadn't been ten minutes? He turned it off more roughly than usual and hauled himself out of bed. He hadn't worked at all yesterday and would have a lot of dissatisfied clients if he didn't sort out their mortgages and insurances before Christmas; he could almost see his pending tray beckoning him. He slid his feet into the cosy sheepskin slippers he'd bought himself as an early festive gift and felt very slightly better. Still clad in his warm tartan pyjamas, not yet up to getting dressed, he padded off toward the kettle making only one stop, to the bathroom, on his route.

Two spoonfuls of coffee and full fat milk ticked all the right boxes and he felt almost human when twenty minutes later after a shower and shave he opened his laptop. He promised himself that if he did three solid hours of work he could then have the reward of making a phone call to Jane on the pretext of discussing the new Roxanne plan. Three hours seemed a long time, maybe two hours would be fairer; after all, he had taken yesterday off for poor Hugo so deserved the treat of talking to Jane. He felt like a love struck puppy; whilst he knew that she was only spending time with him because of Sara and that he was going to get himself hurt, he couldn't seem to stop himself falling for her.

....

Ed and Julia Blackthorpe were on their way to London after having managed to leave the house only five minutes later than their scheduled time. The built in satellite navigation system had said the journey would take two and a quarter hours so Ed calculated that if he made hay while the sun shone and put his foot down on the motorway, the delay from the inevitable but post rush hour traffic should be all but cancelled out. Julia could hardly contain her excitement at a day shopping in a large mall; it was over two years since she'd been to London and she didn't even have feel guilty or worry about getting behind with the Christmas preparations because she'd been very organised and decorated the house three days previously. This year they were spending the 25th and 26th at Ed's sister's in Bath so there wasn't even any food to buy and their two sons, Steven and Ryan weren't arriving till the day before New Year's Eve so she could just relax, browse and choose the boys' presents at her leisure; she sighed contentedly. Whilst she understood that the boys had their own lives, she missed them terribly and couldn't wait to see them. She derived a lot of pleasure though from knowing that the siblings had remained close emotionally even if not geographically.   They often took their annual leave together, habitually in the Canaries and this Christmas they were travelling to the Lanzarote. She and Ed had never been abroad; her husband didn't fancy the food but hoped that one day they might join them. Though Julia had a slight hankering for a foreign holiday, she considered herself very lucky that now Ed was retired, she could spend nearly every day with him. It had been an odd life being married to a copper; always taking second place, never knowing if he would come home safely if at all. Their sons had followed in their father's footsteps, predictably joining the police force and were both rapidly striding up the ranks; she wasn't surprised that though both had had several girlfriends, not one of these women had chosen to be a police wife. In her opinion, modern women weren't as understanding or as happy to sacrifice their own lives as they had been in her day.

Julia had made a flask of tea and brought ginger biscuits and Jaffa cakes for the journey; she had originally packed mince pies but realising how crumbly and difficult they'd be for Ed to eat whilst driving had left them, wrapped in foil, for their supper after Aladdin this evening.

Her husband relaxed back into his heated seat and smiled. He enjoyed driving the Volvo; it was a few years old now but his last one had been going strong with well over two hundred thousand miles on the clock when he'd traded it in for this much newer model. He also enjoyed having the opportunity to make his wife happy and, after thirty-five years of marriage he was familiar enough with her to know that a few hours alone in a shopping mall in London was one of the best luxuries he could give her.

....

Roxanne was jolted awake from a dream about knights and dragons, by a tap at the door. She lay there, initially confused, having no clue where she was before the bizarre events of the previous night started slowly filtering back. Wow, this place was the bees' knees! She heard a man's voice quietly calling.

"Sara, are you awake?"

Sara? Hugo of course! This was all really crazy. She looked round; it had been dark last night and she'd been really tired so hadn't seen the room properly. It was some place with its beautiful long drapes at the sash windows, a lovely old iron fireplace, a rocking chair, a chaise longue and quilted eiderdown on her king size bed.

"Sara!" apparently Hugo wasn't a patient man, she smiled. Oops! She started toward the door and then recognising that she shouldn't greet him naked, grabbed a white silk dressing gown from the top of an ornate bedding box and flung open the panelled door.

"Morning, sorry I was sound asleep and was all confused for a minute. Blimey, this place is posh isn't it?"

Hugo had clearly showered and shaved and just as obviously had not slept well. He was still gorgeous!

"Thanks." Was all he could manage. He had felt bad enough before he had seen this vision of a stranger in Sara's robe that mocked and taunted him. Then;

"Please get dressed. Sara's, er, your clothes are in the wardrobe and drawers." He pointed vaguely. "Oh, and sorry but please don't talk if you don't mind, we can't have Rupert hearing your voice."

"Sure," she whispered hoarsely, giving a little cough, "I've lost my voice anyway with this silly cold". She smiled proudly at her idea and he nodded acknowledging the improvisation.

"Look, this is rather embarrassing but can I give you this for helping? Is it enough?" He handed her a few twenty pound notes sheepishly.

"More than enough!" she croaked rather convincingly "If you're sure? I really don't mind helping for nothing. You've given me a bed and food."

"Of course, I'm awfully grateful, thank you. There's a bathroom with everything you should need just opposite here." he gestured. "I'll come back for you in three quarters of an hour, if that's ok? Sara never rose early anyway." The question was clearly rhetorical because with that he was gone.

. . . .

Jane was pacing. She'd had three cups of tea, eaten five shortbread tails and even vacuumed the entire house; she was doing anything and everything to stop herself phoning Jonathan. Her fingers had hovered over her Samsung several times and it was harder to resist each time. Maybe it wouldn't appear too bad if she called him now; she could say she needed to talk to him about Sara...if she could think of something to say about Sara...if her brain didn't feel like mush. Would it look really weak if she said she just wanted to talk about yesterday because she still felt bad about letting Hugo down? She stared at the screen of her Galaxy losing the strength not to call when it made her physically jump by ringing; the photograph she'd sneakily taken of Jonathan in the pub next to the theatre, filled the screen.

"Hi" she said, too excited to say anymore.

"Hi" she could hear in his voice he felt the same "I, er, wondered if you'd like a coffee. I'm not quite as busy as I thought I would be and am, er, at a bit of a loose end."

She knew he was lying and that he had been thinking up an excuse all morning; she had to use all her self control not to shriek out loud with exhilaration.

"Sure, same place as yesterday in fifty minutes?" cool as a cucumber, she high fived the air silently and then rushed round like a crazy thing getting ready whilst trying to look like she hadn't made such an effort.

Jonathan was already there waiting when she entered the warm cafe; sitting with a mug of coffee attempting unsuccessfully to look nonchalant, pretending to read a newspaper. Jane grinned to herself; knowing that he was as untogether about this as she, gave her confidence a well needed boost and she was able to stroll over, almost casually to join him.

"Hi, I'll just get my coffee and'll be back in a minute." She smiled sweetly, turning away toward the counter, enjoying herself. He leapt up before she had time to reach her destination and took out his wallet.

"I invited you so I'm paying" his eyes twinkled "and we may as well order cake too, don't you think?"

"My mother has always told me to pay my own way and not accept gifts from strange men" she was shocked with herself for flirting so outrageously.

"Then your mother is a very wise woman and I promise to try my best not to be too strange."
She pondered over this and what drink and cake she'd like, then replied compromisingly.

"Then that would be very kind of you and I accept...as long as I pay next time, ok?" She looked up at him shyly and they both knew that her accepting both the drink and that there would be a 'next time' had shifted the dynamics of their relationship.

They chatted for over an hour about the previous day's events and then about their own lives, both disclosing information that helped form their growing bond. They joyfully discovered that they shared the same sense of humour and at one point laughed so hard that people from nearby tables turned round and stared. Poignantly though, they both acknowledged that they felt guilty for enjoying themselves so much when their friend was in such turmoil. They resolved that when Jonathan called Hugo later to find out about how it had gone with Roxy, he would arrange that the three, or now four of them if Hugo felt it fitting, should meet up for a meal and progress report. They decided Jonathan should phone him on his way home straight after their meeting, ostensibly because the conversation would be more private but both knowing that it was really because neither of them wanted to lose even a phone call's length of time from their liaison. Having decided that, their consciences were salved the two now had another meeting to look forward to.

After a little more banter and teasing, Jonathan admitted he really had rather a lot of work to complete and promising to inform the other if they heard anything from Hugo, they bid each other au revoir. As they parted, he also admitted in lowered tones, that getting to know her better had been lovely and he couldn't remember feeling so happy. Gently she placed her hand on his arm, squeezed softly and conceded that she felt the same way. He covered her delicate hand with his much larger one and for a long moment closed his fingers over hers.

. . . .

Roxanne looked at the notes in her hand; £100! This was the best day ever!! She opened the bathroom door and whistled softly at the opulence. She'd really fallen on her feet here and wondered why on earth this Sara, whose clone she luckily seemed to be, had walked away from this; she most certainly shouldn't have. No way would Roxy have ever left such a gorgeous, rich boyfriend and this incredible house. Still, Sara's loss was her, albeit temporary, gain and she intended to make the absolute most of it while she could; she would try her hardest to string this 'job' out as long as possible. Her doppleganger must be unbelievably rich, spoilt, in demand or nuts.

Even though Roxanne would have loved a long dip in the huge sumptuous gold telephone tapped bath, with lots of bubbles out of one of the pretty coloured glass bottles, she knew a shower would be much quicker. Hopefully she'd get a chance to soak in the tub later. She dropped the robe and stepped into the huge glass walled shower and tried to figure out the controls. Suddenly, a cascade of water sprang out from the walls and above her and she was surrounded by little led lights. This was truly heavenly like one the spas she'd seen in the glossy magazines they'd had in the hairdressers her mother had taken her to as a teenager. She couldn't afford a hair cut anymore, let alone a spa day; laughing at herself, she pushed the silly thought away and luxuriantly lathered her hair and body with Sara's very expensive products and gave her mane a much needed conditioning treatment.

Having finished her ablutions, Roxanne wrapped herself in the thick white fluffy towel she found hanging on the gold hook next to the glass wall of the shower enclosure. She quickly towel dried her hair and smothered herself in an apricot and almond body butter before padding back into the bedroom to find a hair dryer and some clothes. The hair dryer was easy, top drawer of the dressing table, so she dried her hair first. More than satisfied with locks that looked shinier than they had for years she hoped that someday soon she'd be able to justify spending money on decent hair stuff; it just showed you got what you paid for. She opened the heavy wardrobe door and searched for something to wear. She felt funny wearing someone else's underwear but she hadn't any clean pants left in her rucksack and Hugo had said to help herself. Sara obviously didn't shop in the same places as she did, these clothes hadn't come from the charity shops and market stalls Roxanne frequented. The thought of the spoilt little rich girl poking around in the Hospice Care store caused her laugh out loud before stifling it, realising it wouldn't have sounded the same as her double's. Sara must have been minted to leave all this stuff; her clothes were simple, stylish, elegant and all made of luxury materials, even her knickers were pure silk! This house was much warmer than she was used to but not as warm as she would have liked, so she chose a long green velvet skirt and a high necked cream sweater. A green and peach scarf was hanging over the skirt so presumably Sara must have worn them together. She circled the swathes of material around her neck and caught it with a beautiful gold and pearl brooch that she found on the dressing table. Her trainers didn't quite go with this ensemble and as it appeared they fortunately shared the same size, she donned a pair of low comfortable leather boots and, for completeness, a Mulberry leather handbag. Fun as it was, she felt guilty about participating in this charade when it was such a waste of poor Hugo's time and the farce was just prolonging his pain but despite this she couldn't help selfishly enjoying it. Roxanne didn't possess any makeup of her own but, seeing as she were playing dress-up and still had a few minutes of the forty-five left, she put on a smearing of Sara's peachy lipstick and a little blusher. Having gone this far and still having heard no sign of Hugo, she put a couple of coats of the Mac brown mascara on too. As Sara had left all this stuff and it was no longer wanted, maybe, when he came to terms with things, Hugo might let her keep some of it. She realised she'd already got far too carried away with this fantasy but if she could daydream about clothes and make up, perhaps she could allow herself to dream she could have Hugo too. Probably fortunately, her daydream was interrupted before she could go any further.

"Sara?" Hugo's voice came from the open doorway.

"Come in, I'm decent." She giggled quietly and then realising her insensitivity said "I'm sorry, Hugo, truly I am, that was a silly thing to say, this all just feels so unreal to me."

He came into the room but upon seeing her, turned immediately away, brushing, what Roxanne figured, must be a tear from his face.

"I really am sorry." she repeated. "This must be very hard for you, me looking so much like her and all." She gently placed her hand on his arm. "What's the plan?" He instinctively and immediately flinched away before recovering enough to answer.

"I think we should keep it simple and just go and sit in the lounge, like Sara and I always did, and wait for Rupert to see us. Now you're wearing her clothes, as long as you carry on with the croaky whisper he'll without doubt think that you're Sara. As Jane says, it ought to be easy because we'll be able to see straight away from his reaction if he knows anything about her disappearance."

"And then what?" she asked logically.

"That's the problem, I'm not really sure." he said flatly. "I'm still not at all convinced this has got anything to do with Rupert; we may be making a ridiculous mistake but I guess if it's clear he isn't to blame then we'll just have to team up with Jonathan and Jane again and investigate further to find out who the hell has taken her..." He paused, blinking away more tears. "If he looks shocked and therefore had everything to do with her abduction, then we'll just have to get out of the house quickly and, again, meet the others. Jane will know what to do, won't she?"

Sara looked down. This poor deluded guy was in cloud cuckoo land. How could he even consider that his friend and employee of several years had stolen away his girlfriend and done what with her? Sold her into slavery? The whole idea was ludicrous and the sooner they got this whole Rupert thing over with, the better. Not knowing what to say, she simply nodded with as much seriousness as she could muster.

Hugo was relieved that she seemed to be getting the hang of not talking and that he didn't have to further endure the freakiness of listening to an alien accent emitting from Sara. In silence the two of them walked slowly down the stairs together and Roxanne, free of the rush of last night, was able to see that the whole place was as at least as plush as her bedroom and bathroom. She admired the deep pile claret coloured carpet, dark wood banisters, gilt framed paintings and huge pot plants; it was more like a film set than a house. To the manor born or what?! Hugo led her into the front room where she was glad to see a real log fire roaring. The room slightly reminded her of the assembly hall of her old school with its parquet flooring and heavy, full length curtains, only these were gorgeous velvet and the wood floor was partially covered with a massive oriental looking rug. They sat down awkwardly together on the velvet settee.

Chapter Twenty-One

Jonathan turned his collar up against the cold wind and was grateful he was wearing his phone gloves so he didn't need to call bare handed. He tried to wipe the permanent but now inappropriate grin off his face and called his friend. His first attempt went to voicemail after seven rings, and his second and five minutes later, his third. Hugo's phone must be on silent or he was simply too preoccupied to answer it; he'd try again when he got home.

....

At just after half past ten, Blackthorpe dropped an excited Julia off at Westfields with his credit card and her mobile phone. They had already arranged that he would call her when he'd finished and that they would have an early dinner at her choice of one of the many eateries in the mall. Waving to his practically skipping wife, he keyed the post code and house number from the business card the woman had given him into the sat nav.

Fifty minutes later he eventually drew into a parking space at a car park near enough to the square. He felt like a bit of a walk after the couple of stressful altercations he'd had with his know it all but inept electronic guide; it always insisted it was right even when Blackthorpe, who was on the spot after all, could clearly see that the road layout had changed since the damn thing's last update. To compound his disenchantment, once it had frustratingly slowly recalculated, after he had probably missed several completely suitable turnings and was several blocks further along, it had sent him back the same blasted way. By the third attempt, he had felt like throwing the bloody thing out of the window, giving up and going to a pub till his wife had had her fill of the shops; instead he had merely impotently sworn very loudly and very obscenely at the inanimate object. He really mustn't allow these things to unsettle him so much, Julia was always telling him so; she would have reasoned a sat nav was only a dumb machine and it had made the journey as a whole much easier than it would have been if they'd had to navigate using a map like they'd done before its invention.

....

Jonathan redialled Hugo's number again with no luck. After another couple of failed attempts at rousing his friend he became sufficiently concerned to abandon the jobs that had become rather urgent and call round to the square in person. He was sure everything would be alright but he didn't like not hearing from Hugo just in case things had gone badly with Rupert. He easily persuaded himself that Jane wouldn't like to be left out and called her with the update straight away. Her voice sounded even more worried than he'd expected so he arranged to pick her up en route, as her house was only a ten minute detour; they could make plans as they drove over together.

....

Rupert thought he heard footsteps and made his way into the hall, maybe today would be the day Hugo finally saw sense. Four days seemed to him to be more than enough time for anyone to get over their mourning period. As he walked through the hall he heard and smelt that the fire had been lit in the main reception room and was pleased that this must be a positive step toward Hugo's rehabilitation. He popped his head into the lounge and was about to call an encouraging 'good morning' when he was stopped dead in his tracks. Hugo was not alone; he was with Sara. Rupert stood motionless, prepared for fight or flight; how could this be? His head spun as he struggled to comprehend the situation. He felt like he was in some sort of time slip. He fought to clear his thoughts. Hugo must have somehow discovered and revived her and that meant by now she would have told him everything and they would have already rung the police. He had to get out of here quickly and quietly but his legs felt too numb to carry him and his eyes seemed morbidly glued to the couple.

The two lovers were both sitting, staring directly into the fire and very unusually for them, not interacting, not even touching. Rupert knew it was crazy but it occurred to him that this could actually be Sara's ghost and maybe he was the only one who could see her. Could it have come back here to taunt and haunt him for what he had done to her? Despite the roaring fire, he felt cold. His mind raced but before he could settle and arrange his thoughts, something must have alerted them to his presence because they both turned toward him in unison. Fight kicked in and he sprang into action grabbing Sara or her ghost by the throat; this solid being was no spectre, what on earth had he been thinking? The nasty little scrap was much feistier than he would have expected after having not eaten or drunk for several days and she nearly managed to break free of him by kicking her boot heel back into his shin.

Hugo lunged toward them but Rupert was quicker, darting back and tightening his grip round her neck. Hugo hesitated, clearly understanding that his approach would cause more danger to her.

Suddenly the evil she-devil started shouting and hissing in what his deranged mind could only think might be in tongues and again Rupert questioned if she were in fact something paranormal. It was several seconds before Rupert worked out that what he was hearing was, in fact, a strong Birmingham accent and a few more seconds before his brain connected that this fiend was indeed human but was not Sara! He felt giddy; Hugo had somehow tricked him; obviously the man who he had thought of as his master was not the fair and kind man he had believed him to be. Rupert dragged the thrashing frame of whoever this was toward the rear porch and transferring her neck to the crook of his elbow to free a hand, struggled but succeeded in unlocking the cellar door.

He flung it open as Hugo, who had been poised not knowing what to do for the best, just a second too late, seized his opportunity and threw himself at the abductor. Rupert neatly side stepped and deflected Hugo's trajectory through the door and swiftly shut and locked it behind him as his wretched prey half flew, half stumbled down the stairwell into the darkness. Meanwhile, the squirming rat twisted her neck and bit down into his forearm drawing blood; Christ, Hugo had the most appalling choice in women. He winced and jabbed her sharply in the stomach with his fist, quietening her long enough to drag her winded body after him into the study. The last thing he wanted in his personal space or indeed in his life was this hideous little demon but, if Hugo had somehow discovered what had happened to Sara and the police had been informed, then he needed this mirror image as an insurance policy to trick the authorities into thinking Sara was still fit and well. The police would only have had a photo, at the most, so the voice that was even worse than Sara's wine shouldn't be a problem. Rupert was working purely on guesswork and didn't have a clear plan but knew he needed to get away from the house as soon as possible; having to talk to and deflect the plod was something he really could not be bothered with today. It was tiresome that he didn't have time to pack but he possessed very little and nothing that he couldn't exist without or afford to replace. He'd had his fill of this place and fortunately being able to lead a life after Redcliffe square wasn't going to be a burden for him; he had been wisely frugal with his wages and built up funds that could keep him for quite some time. In any case, he was confident that even without a reference he could easily find satisfactory employment if and when he required it.

. . . .

Hugo had launched himself gallantly toward the stricken Roxanne, planning to save her and disable Rupert long enough to get help but instead he found himself hurtling into the terrifyingly oppressive chamber below the house...into his worst nightmare. How could his carefully timed leap have backfired so badly and with such horrifying consequences? He landed with a massively painful thud bounce thud and felt what must be blood trickling down his forehead. Even the searing pain from the instantaneously growing bump on the front of his head wasn't sufficient to fight back his equally growing terror of the enclosed space. He couldn't breathe. He couldn't think straight. His heart felt like it would pound free of his body. The walls were pressing in toward him and squeezing the air from him; he felt light headed and dizzy and sick. No. He had to take control; he had to concentrate. His phone contained a torch and hopefully, down here, a signal to call for help; he reached into his pocket and realised with an intense pain and involuntary moan that his right arm must be broken.

With great effort, he reached round with his left hand and discovered hopelessly that the screen of his phone had smashed. He found and optimistically pressed the 'on' button but his positivity was not rewarded and his attempts were futile. The claustrophobia that would have debilitated him in the light was worse in this confining darkness and threatened to completely engulf him. His ever more hammering heart felt like it was going to burst into his mouth as he gasped to take in the oxygen that eluded him; he squeezed his thumbnail into the flesh of his forefinger and for the first time in longer than he could remember, he prayed. His breathing calmed just enough to enable him to draw himself to a painful upright, shuffling blind, holding onto the wine rack that he had fallen against for orientation to try and find a light switch. If he hadn't been so stupidly stubborn and gone to see Jane for this incapacitating phobia when Jonathan had first recommended her this would be so much less distressing; he only had himself to blame.

Before he had managed more than a couple of tentative steps, he stumbled and tripped over something which fortunately broke his fall sufficiently for him to remember to reach out with his undamaged arm. In the darkness he ran his able hand over the pile of smelly, damp material and discovered to his sickening horror that he had found someone lying there in the darkness. He recoiled in terror and disgust, his mind numb, for a stricken moment not wanting to know more, not daring to check, not wanting his very worst fears confirmed.

He had to know. He smoothed his hand over the skin of the neck and felt the delicate features of a female face and what was left of the gag, his fingers stroked the long silken hair; Sara's hair.

Howling powerlessly into the blackness he gently and then more roughly shook her motionless and unresponsive body against the restraints, retching, despite himself at the stench of always clean and fragrant body. He whimpered her name over and over, unable to even begin to imagine the terror and pain she must have felt. He forced himself to be practical; whilst he desperately wanted to free and hold her, his priority had to be reviving her terrifyingly still and seemingly lifeless little body; he hated himself for his impotence. This was all his stupid, stupid fault; he had been an absolute imbecile allowing Rupert, evil, evil Rupert to 'search' down here for her. Again he castigated himself for his weakness at not sorting out his phobia earlier; he should have searched his own bloody cellar. Only a complete fool would have been such a bad judge of character to trust that monster. And why had he been so blinkeredly sure that Sara had been taken away from the house? He was as culpable as Rupert for causing his angel this much suffering. He was supposed to be her protector; had believed he could marry her but he had never deserved or been worthy of her or indeed anything. This was his punishment for being so pathetic; this is what he deserved.

Dragging his tattered self together, he saw that whilst he had been the biggest moron ever, at least he could try to help her now. He dredged through his memories for the CPR training he'd once received on a first aid course and pushed the heel of his able right hand down onto her chest relentlessly; again and again and again and again he pumped, checking regularly for signs of life, pain coursing through his own body, sobbing uncontrollably until, eventually, he detected a very weak but perceptible pulse in her limply unconscious body.

. . . .

Rupert hauled his new captive into the study with difficulty. Though she was light, overpowering the aggressively writhing and screeching witch was a challenge but finally, despite her flailing limbs he managed to tug on Hugo's warm camel coat and sheepskin hat without any more of his bloodshed. He acknowledged that the private rooms that had been his home were no longer his but he was glad that he had no need to taint them with the *thing* he was holding. He was seriously fed up with the inconvenience of her and taking

141

Hugo's ornate brass letter opener from the desk hissed at her threateningly to shut the fuck up, stop fighting and walk out calmly with him or he would happily welcome having an excuse to plunge the surprisingly sharp knife into her scrawny little neck.

Roxanne was very frightened but was even more angry; how dare he think he could get away with hurting people without retribution. She twisting her head round sharply again, this time sinking her teeth into his cheek. He yelped pathetically, flashing his weirdly wild eyes at her before punching a person's face for the first time in his life; he immediately and desperately wanted to cleanse his sullied hand. He wished he could kill her but needed the bitch alive. She gasped at the stinging pain of the thump and realised furiously that she had no choice other than to tow the line till she could find another chance of attacking him or escaping his grip. The madness in his soulless eyes told her that he couldn't possibly be reasoned with and she knew she wouldn't be able to help Hugo and the girlfriend she had unfairly maligned if she provoked him into killing her. She would have to bide her time and pray that an opportunity would present itself outside where, judging by the coat and hat Hugo had been wearing yesterday, they were heading.

. . . .

It wasn't much above freezing but Roxanne was too aware of the sharp brass tool being pushed hard against her throat to notice that she was outside in December without a coat. It only took the smallest movement of the paper knife to steer her down the steps and to the right along the pavement. She wasn't terribly good at doing what she was told at the best of times and this was most definitely not the best of times. She *hated* having to be subservient to this bully; she could feel the rebellious teenager within her beginning to overshadow the frightened child. She must temper this though because it was precisely that 'I'll do what I want and 'I know it all'' attitude that had got her into this mess in the first place. She could never just go along with the crowd; she was the one who had been pregnant in a school uniform, the poor but invincible one hitch-hiking her way round the country. The other three musketeers had been right all

142

along and she now bitterly wished she hadn't been so much of a smart-ass not to have taken them seriously. She was proving to be an even worse judge of character than she had imagined; she had put both Hugo and herself in danger. If she hadn't been so wrapped up in her own stuff she could have somehow been prepared for this, armed herself with a weapon of some kind; even a perfume spray would have afforded her some time. Having a 999 pre-dialled phone in her hand would have been a Godsend but no, she had known better. This had started out as such a good day; she remembered all the money in the Mulberry handbag that must still be on Hugo's settee; funny what thoughts came into your mind at times like these. She wanted nothing more than to dig her heel into his shin again and follow it with a knee where it would hurt most but he wasn't loosening his grip one iota and the surprisingly sharp metal point was pressing to firmly into the skin beneath Sara's beautiful and no doubt very expensive scarf.

. . . .

Blackthorpe arrived at Redcliffe Square on foot, happy to get a break from his electronic friend, and was struck immediately by the impressiveness of the neighbourhood; an apartment here must be worth over a million pounds and the address on Hugo's card showed that he did not just live in a section of a house. These people were certainly not short of a bob or two; crime was often no respecter of class or wealth. The ex copper's head was swimming with questions and ideas that he wanted to discuss with the wannabe but probably well meaning detectives as he strode purposefully, cold hands thrust deep into his pockets, breath visible in the crisp air.

He was just yards away and in clear sight of the door he'd worked out to be the correct one, when he saw a man he recognised as Hugo from the coat and hat he'd been wearing the night before with his arm protectively around the shoulders of the very slim Sara of the photograph; her long pale blond hair cascading over her coatless back. He would never understand these girls; his daughter was the same despite having a wardrobe of warm outerwear.

143

Furiously, he watched the pair shut the door behind them and turn to walk away from him, nauseatingly infatuated; their silly heads touching. He could barely believe he had wasted all this time and energy on such a fickle and immature bunch of youngsters; he seethed inwardly for having allowed himself to get embroiled in their domestic quarrel. In other circumstances he would have been pleased to find that two lovers had been reunited, but right now he felt used and stupid and very, very much like he wanted to punch something. To avoid any possibility of that unwanted scenario, he turned sharply on his heels with only an argument with the bloody sat nav and being dragged round the shops for hours on end to look forward to. He groaned sardonically; fabulous, his life was complete.

The End

#0220 - 210116 - C0 - 210/148/0 - PB - DID1334752